"This is between my son and me,"

Irene said.

"He seems to have included me in it." Murdock took a step closer. "Your son has decided he wants a father and he seems to think I would be a good choice."

"I'm really sorry he's been nagging you," she managed, then marveled that the sentence had come out coherently. There was a heat in his eyes that could melt a snowcap, she thought, feeling her shield turn to slush.

She started to edge her way toward the door. Murdock placed a hand against the wall, blocking her retreat with his arm. "I'm flattered he thinks so highly of me. He's a terrific kid."

Murdock leaned closer to her. His warm breath teased her skin. "I've been thinking that a man would be proud to have Jeremy for a son." His gaze bore into her. "And that you have the most kissable lips...."

Dear Reader,

Silhouette Romance rings in the New Year with a great new FABULOUS FATHER from bestselling author Elizabeth August! Murdock Parnell may be the *Ideal Dad* for eight-year-old Jeremy Galvin, but will he convince Jeremy's pretty mom, Irene, that he's her ideal husband?

In Kristin Morgan's latest book, Brianna Stansbury is *A Bride To Be*. Problem is, her groom-to-be is up to no good. It's up to Drew Naquin to rescue Brianna—even if that means marrying her himself!

Expectant Bachelor concludes Sandra Steffen's heartwarming WEDDING WAGER series about three brothers who vow they'll never say "I do." This time, Taylor Harris must battle the forces of love. And once he discovers the woman in his arms plans to be the mother of his child, it's not easy.

Rounding out the month, Carol Grace brings us a *Lonely Millionaire* who's looking for a mail-order bride. Liz Ireland turns up the laughter when a young woman finds herself playing *Mom for a Week*—with only her long-ago love to rescue her. And look for *The Man Who Changed Everything* from debut author Elizabeth Sites.

Until next month,

Happy reading!

Anne Canadeo
Senior Editor

Please address questions and book requests to:
Silhouette Reader Service
U.S.: 3010 Walden Ave., P.O. Box 1325, Buffalo, NY 14269
Canadian: P.O. Box 609, Fort Erie, Ont. L2A 5X3

ELIZABETH AUGUST

IDEAL DAD

Silhouette
ROMANCE™
Published by Silhouette Books
America's Publisher of Contemporary Romance

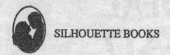

SILHOUETTE BOOKS

ISBN 0-373-19054-9

IDEAL DAD

Copyright © 1995 by Elizabeth August

Printed in U.S.A.

Books by Elizabeth August

Silhouette Romance

Author's Choice #554
Truck Driving Woman #590
Wild Horse Canyon #626
Something So Right #668
The Nesting Instinct #719
Joey's Father #749
Ready-Made Family #771
The Man from Natchez #790
A Small Favor #809
The Cowboy and the Chauffeur #833
Like Father, Like Son #857
The Wife He Wanted #881
*The Virgin Wife #921
*Haunted Husband #922
*Lucky Penny #945
*A Wedding for Emily #953
*The Seeker #989
†The Forgotten Husband #1019
†Ideal Dad #1054

Silhouette Special Edition

One Last Fling! #871

*Smytheshire, Massachusetts Series
†Where The Heart Is

ELIZABETH AUGUST

lives in western North Carolina, with her husband, Doug, and her three boys, Douglas, Benjamin and Matthew. She began writing romances soon after Matthew was born. She's always wanted to write.

Elizabeth does counted cross-stitching to keep from eating at night. It doesn't always work. "I love to bowl, but I'm not very good. I keep my team's handicap high. I like hiking in the Shenandoahs, as long as we start up the mountain so the return trip is down rather than vice versa." She loves to go to Cape Hatteras to watch the sun rise over the ocean.

Elizabeth August has also published books under the pseudonym Betsy Page.

Murdock Parnell on Fatherhood...

From the first day Jeremy entered my life, I've admired his spirit. I knew he was afraid of me; still, he was determined to protect his mother against me if the need arose. And when I offered him my hand in apology for frightening him, even though I could tell he continued to be intimidated by me, he stepped up and shook it.

But what has truly surprised me is my reaction to the boy. I came here seeking solitude. However, instead of resenting his intrusions, I've found myself enjoying his company and actually looking forward to our "man-to-man" talks. It's also become obvious to me that he thinks I'd make a good father for him. And I find myself wanting to fulfill that role.

I realize being a stepfather won't be easy. But, instead of thinking of myself as his stepdad, I'd think of myself as his "second dad." And, I would treat him as if he were my true son, because in my heart and mind, he would be.

Now all I have to do is convince his mother that I'm the right husband for her as well as the ideal father for Jeremy.

Chapter One

"What's ya using for bait, mister?"

Murdock Parnell looked over his shoulder to see a young boy, around eight years of age, he judged, standing on the pier behind him. He'd thought he would be left totally alone up here at the Brockman's place, situated as it was on a secluded lake in this heavily forested region of Minnesota. Admittedly Horace had mentioned a caretaker and he'd given Murdock a number to call in case of an emergency. And, earlier today, when he'd driven up the long private, gravel road that had ended at the Brockman house, Murdock had noticed a small two-story residence nestled among a stand of pines about a mile back.

But Horace hadn't mentioned a child. The frown that had seemed to ingrain itself into Murdock's features during the past days, grew grimmer. "Haven't your parents taught you it's not safe to talk to strangers?" he demanded curtly.

Fear showed on the boy's face and he took a step backward.

The pier was long but narrow. As the boy took a second step back, Murdock noticed he was going more sideways than backward. Another movement of retreat would land the child in the water. "Stop," he ordered, and made a grab for the boy.

"Mom!" the child shrieked. Barely avoiding Murdock's grasp, he whirled around. To Murdock's relief he chose the direction that did not land him in water. In the next instant, the boy raced off the pier and up the gravel path that led to the house.

Murdock groaned. He hadn't meant to really scare the child. "Well, at least, he'll think twice about talking to strangers," he muttered under his breath, trying to alleviate his guilt by convincing himself he'd done a good deed.

His gaze shifted back to the blue-green water of the lake. Horace had said he'd have his caretaker stock the refrigerator. It had been bare when Murdock had arrived today but then he hadn't been expected until tomorrow. Obviously the caretaker's wife had arrived with the groceries and brought her son along.

Murdock frowned indecisively. Should he go up to the house and introduce himself or stay here and fish? Stay here and fish, he decided. It was already late afternoon and that meant there wouldn't be much sunlight left. Besides, he'd accepted Horace's offer of this wilderness retreat in search of solitude.

Remembering he'd cast his line into the water just before the boy arrived, he reeled it in, then cast it out again.

Irene Orman Galvin strode down the gravel path, fire in her eyes. Nobody bullied her son and got away with it! Coming to an abrupt halt at the beginning of the pier, she glared at the man standing near the other end. She hadn't tried to be silent and as he finished reeling in his line, he turned to see who had approached.

"If you're not Murdock Parnell you'd better get off this land," she ordered. The thought that her and what army were going to move him if he wasn't and didn't want to go, abruptly played through her mind. Jeremy had been adamant in warning her that the man was big. When her son had described him as a match for a grizzly bear, she'd been sure he'd been exaggerating. Every adult looked large to an eight-year-old.

Now, she realized Jeremy had been a little excessive but not by much in his description. The man at the end of the pier was a couple of inches over six feet tall. To protect against the brisk September breeze, he wore a heavy blue flannel shirt under a bulky sweater. But even taking into consideration the thickness of his clothing, his shoulders were broad. His jeans hugged sturdily built thighs. And, she had the distinct impression that none of his bulk was flab.

Jeremy hadn't been exaggerating about the man's face, either. With that scowl, he did look scary. Her back stiffened. There had been a time when she could be intimidated by a mere look but that had been a lifetime ago. Her gaze narrowed threateningly.

"I am Murdock Parnell," he said. "I know you weren't expecting me until Saturday but I decided to take an extra day off."

She saw the hint of an indulgent smile at one corner of his mouth. So he thought her anger was humorous, she fumed, her ire rising. "You may enjoy frightening small children, Mr. Parnell, but don't you ever try to grab my son again."

Murdock's scowl returned. "I was trying to keep him from backing off the pier into the water."

Irene saw the man's gaze shift from her to something behind her. Glancing over her shoulder, she saw Jeremy a few feet up the path, watching the confrontation. "I thought I told you to wait in the car," she said sternly.

His posture stiffened and a protectiveness came over his features. "I thought you might need help," he replied, approaching her.

She noticed his gaze had rested on her only momentarily. As he walked, he'd turned his attention back to the man on the pier. Looking at Murdock Parnell, she saw his full attention was on her son and there was apology on his face.

"I'm sorry I was so gruff," Murdock said as Jeremy came to a halt beside her. "You surprised me. I thought I was alone here."

There was no hint of patronization in his voice when he spoke, Irene noticed with surprise. Instead he addressed her son as an equal.

"My mom did tell me I wasn't supposed to bother you," Jeremy admitted, studying Murdock with cautious curiosity.

"Then we both owe each other an apology," Murdock replied, extending his hand toward the boy.

For a moment Jeremy hesitated, then, his back straight with courage, he approached Murdock and shook the man's hand. But as if not completely assured Murdock was safe to be around, he quickly returned to his mother's side.

Irene had to admit Mr. Parnell's remorse for having scared her son seemed genuine. She also recalled that Horace Brockman had expressed an admiration for the man and Horace wasn't a person who could be fooled by outward appearances. Still, Murdock Parnell made her uneasy. "I've stocked your refrigerator with the necessities. There are also some snack foods in the pantry and the meats and packs of seafood in the freezer are all marked. I generally come on Mondays to clean the place. If you need it cleaned before then, let me know. My name's Irene Galvin and my phone number is the one at the top of the emergency list on the wall by the phone. Also, if anything needs to be repaired, call me," she instructed in businesslike tones. Taking her son's hand, she added, "Good day, Mr. Parnell," and began walking back in the direction of the house.

Murdock knew when he'd been given the cold shoulder. He frowned at himself as he watched the woman and child walk away. He'd come up here to relax, not make enemies of the caretaker's wife and child. The boy glanced back at him and he grinned and winked in a second show of apology. The lingering apprehension that had been in the boy's eyes faded and a tiny smile flickered on the child's face.

Well, maybe the child didn't consider him the enemy but the wife sure did, he thought as he walked back to the end of the pier and cast his line in once again.

He told himself to forget them, but their images stayed strong in his mind. It was easy to see they were mother and son. Both had the same thick black hair and blue eyes. And the cut of their features was similar, from the almond shape of those blue eyes to their small straight noses to their high cheekbones. The woman's lips, however, had been a bit fuller than the boy's. Sensual, actually. Nice curve to her hips too, he added, finding himself picturing her walking away and thinking they'd had an enticing swing to them. Immediately he reminded himself that she was married. And, no doubt she's a real handful for that husband of hers to handle, he speculated. This thought was supposed to illicit a surge of sympathy for the man. Instead Murdock experienced a jab of envy. Frowning at himself, he returned to his mental inspection of the mother and son. All in all, the boy was cute and his mother was pretty... not ravishingly beautiful but pleasant to the eye.

"And neither one of them is of any concern to me," he stated aloud. The only reason they were still on his mind, he assured himself, was that he had a need to assess all people with whom he came in contact. That was part of his personality. But now he'd made his assessment and could put the woman and child out of his mind. "Just one little addition," he murmured under his breath. "I think it would be wise not to call her or her husband unless it's a matter of life or death."

Satisfied, he concentrated on his fishing.

"Stay away from Mr. Parnell," Irene ordered her son as they drove back to their cabin.

"I just surprised him. He didn't mean to be mean," he replied, with an impatient expression that reminded Irene of his father.

"He wants to be left alone," she returned. "I'm asking you to respect his wishes."

Jeremy turned toward the lake. A gap in the trees allowed him to see the man on the pier. "All right," he replied with a hint of disappointment.

Irene glanced at her son out of the corner of her eye. Did he miss having adult male companionship so much he was willing to seek out a boorish stranger? Since his father's death, she'd tried to be both father and mother to him and she'd thought she'd been fairly successful. Well, nobody's perfect, she mused philosophically. Besides, she had some news that would take his mind off Murdock Parnell. "Your great-aunt Sarah's coming to visit. She should be here in time for dinner."

Jeremy jerked his attention back to his mother. "The tall lady who looks sort of scary?"

"She appears intimidating but she isn't," Irene replied, coming to Sarah's defense. "She just has a military bearing because of all the years she was a nurse in the navy."

Jeremy gave her another impatient glance. "I know she's not really scary." Abruptly he grinned. "She let me have pizza with sardines on it for breakfast."

"She would," Irene muttered, thinking that her son certainly lived up to the old proverb that the way to a man's heart was through his stomach. "Oh, no," she groaned. "Aunt Sarah isn't even here and I'm already thinking in adages."

Curiosity replaced Jeremy's grin. "What's an adage?"

"It's a sage saying or a proverb that's supposed to be a fragment of wisdom for living, or something to that effect," she replied. "Aunt Sarah uses them all of the time. For example, a bird in hand is worth two in the bush."

Jeremy frowned in confusion. "I thought you said wild animals were better off free and I wasn't supposed to try to catch them."

Irene groaned mentally. She should never have brought this up. "You're right about wild animals. The adage is just another way of saying you should appreciate what you have."

"I see," he said slowly, clearly not understanding at all. Then shrugging as if to say he'd decided this conversation was irrelevant, he grinned with pride. "When we went fishing, I had to put the worms on Aunt Sarah's hook."

Irene smiled, but the smile turned to a thoughtful frown as her aunt's phone call again played through her mind. Sarah hadn't asked if now would be a convenient time for her to visit. She'd simply stated that she would be arriving this afternoon.

Irene's back muscles tensed. Aunt Sarah had sounded like a woman with a purpose. But then Sarah always sounded like that, she reminded herself and stretched her back to release the tension in the muscles.

* * *

"Jeremy is tucked into bed," Sarah announced with an air of accomplishment as she stepped out onto the porch and eased herself into one of the rocking chairs.

Irene smiled at her from the porch swing. "It really wasn't necessary for you to play a fourth game of checkers with him."

"He's a sweet child. I enjoyed it," Sarah returned. "I recall nights when I played games for hours with you and you still refused to settle down."

Irene's gaze traveled over the woman who now sat rocking and looking out at the lake. Like herself, Sarah's features were somewhat sharply defined. But they blended well. It was the way Sarah wore her hair that gave her a markedly stern appearance. The long tresses, which had once been as ebony as Irene's but were now ever so lightly streaked with gray, were tightly braided and wound around Sarah's head in a spinsterly style. In contrast, there was nothing staid about Sarah's choice in clothes. At the moment she was wearing a flowing summer dress with huge blue flowers on a scarlet background. To provide protection from the chilly night air, she had added a multicolored wool poncho.

"I know this is long past due, but I don't think I've ever properly thanked you," Irene said, speaking aloud the thoughts that had been taunting her for the past hour.

Sarah regarded her quizzically. "Thank me?"

"For helping me find the courage to choose my own path after Jack died," Irene elaborated. "I have to admit, when my mom and dad invited me to come live with them, I considered doing just that. I might have been chronologically nearly twenty-four but I was still closer to eighteen in many ways. The thought of wrapping myself and Jeremy in that safe little cocoon they offered was tempting. But if I'd accepted their offer I might never have learned that I have the strength to survive on my own."

"I'm very proud of the way you've taken care of yourself and Jeremy," Sarah said. "So are your parents. And from what I hear, your in-laws are very pleased as well."

Irene frowned. She knew Sarah meant what she'd just said. However, she'd caught a hint of hesitation in her aunt's voice. "But..." she interjected, letting Sarah know she knew her aunt had more to add.

"But," Sarah continued, "we are all a little concerned that you are taking this independence a bit too far."

Irene's frown deepened. "You're talking about me getting married again."

"Right now, I'm merely talking about you getting out. You're still a young woman. You were just twenty-eight your last birthday. Jack's been gone nearly four years now and, according to your mother, you still aren't dating...at least not so's anyone would notice. I'm not saying you should forget Jack. You have a lot of good memories of your time with him and you should cherish those. But you need to get on with your life."

"I wasn't surprised when I had this conversation with my mother. I wasn't even totally surprised when Jack's mother brought the subject up. She's always treated me like a daughter and both she and my mother have long-standing marriages. They believe a woman needs a husband to be truly happy." Irene regarded her aunt dryly. "But I am shocked at you, Aunt Sarah. Of all the people in our family I thought you would be the one who would know that a woman doesn't have to have a man around to feel fulfilled."

"I may be forty and still unmarried but that doesn't mean I don't believe in looking around to find a man to share your life with. It seems to me that having the right man around could make life a great deal more fun," Sarah replied primly. "And I have the highest regard for the institution of matrimony."

Irene mentally kicked herself. She hadn't meant to upset her aunt. "I know," she said with apology. "You've told me a little about your lost love. Ward, right?" Suddenly seeing a way to win this discussion, she continued hurriedly. "Well, I guess I'm a lot like you . . . I'm a 'one man' woman, too."

"I never said I was a 'one man' woman." A wistfulness entered Sarah's voice. "I've simply never met the right 'other' man. But I intend to keep looking. I figure I'll know him when I see him."

Irene couldn't stop herself from smiling. "You mean bells will ring and you'll hear an orchestra playing?"

Sarah nodded. "Something like that."

"You never fail to amaze me," Irene admitted. "I'd have never guessed you were such a romantic at heart."

Sarah raised an eyebrow. "And I never thought you would become a cynic."

Irene's smile vanished. "I'm not a cynic. I'm simply very happy with my life just the way it is."

Abruptly Sarah's expression became warm and motherly. "Then I'm happy for you. And, we'll declare this discussion closed."

Irene stared at her aunt, hardly believing her ears. When Sarah had called to say she was coming, Irene had been worried that her aunt's visit had been prompted by her mother and that she would have to spend the entire time attempting to convince Sarah she was happy with her life as it was. Recovering from the shock of Sarah's unexpected capitulation, she said with relief, "Thank you."

Sarah's smile warmed even more. "I didn't come here to preach but to visit, take long walks and cook. I hate cooking for one so when I'm home I rarely spend much time in the kitchen. Here I have you and Jeremy to try my recipes out on."

So relieved she wasn't going to have to spend the next days explaining her feelings to her aunt, even the threat of Sarah's cooking didn't bother Irene. "I appreciate that," she replied, gratefully.

Sarah gave her a quirky "I know how difficult families can be" grin, then turned her attention back to the lake and wooded landscape surrounding it. "I see a light on in the Brockman's house," she said. "Maybe I'll walk over tomorrow and say hello to Daisy."

Irene felt her back muscles tensing once again as she followed her aunt's line of vision. "Daisy and Horace aren't there. They've loaned the place to a man by the name of Murdock Parnell."

Sarah continued to gaze lazily across the lake. "What's he like?"

A gigantic nuisance was the first thought that came into Irene's mind. But she stopped herself before she said this aloud. Forcing an indifference into her voice, she replied instead, "I'd guess he's in his early thirties. He's well built, brown hair cut conservatively with a part on the side... brown eyes."

Irene frowned at how vividly she remembered Murdock Parnell. Unexpectedly she found herself comparing him to her late husband. Jack Galvin had been a handsome man. The kind of man women always looked at twice. He'd been captain of the football team and half the girls in school had had crushes on him. During the summer his blond hair would get so bleached out by the sun it was almost white and his blue eyes were the color of a warm summer sky.

"I suppose you could say Mr. Parnell is reasonably good-looking," she conceded aloud. "Well, maybe interesting would be a better description. Well, not exactly interesting

even," she quickly corrected, surprised his image continued to remain strong beside Jack's.

"Sounds like you got a good look at him."

Irene glanced at her aunt to find Sarah studying her
thoughtfully. "He frightened Jeremy. We had a short confrontation. The man's a boor."

Immediately Sarah's expression became that of a mother
hen. "He frightened Jeremy?" she demanded, looking as if
she was ready to go give the man a piece of her mind that
very minute.

"Jeremy startled him. He did apologize," Irene elaborated, then was surprised that she'd been so quick to come
to Mr. Parnell's defense. I'm just being fair, she told herself.

Sarah's expression relaxed and she again turned her attention to the house across the lake. "I suppose he's here on
vacation."

Irene found her own gaze being drawn to the lights across
the water and again she frowned. She didn't want to talk
about Murdock Parnell. The way his image continued to
remain so vivid in her mind made her uneasy. "Yes," she
replied, then determined to change the subject, she jerked
her attention back to Sarah and asked, "Has Eloise completely recovered from that spill she took off her motorcy-
cle? Did all of her memory return?"

Sarah smiled. "Your cousin is going to be right as rain.
And yes, nearly all of her memory has returned. We don't
need to worry about Eloise. That husband of hers might be
a little rough around the edges but I trust him to take real
good care of her. A cur dog once made a friend is a friend
for life."

Her aunt's words touched a sensitive nerve. "She's not a
child. I'm sure she could take good care of herself," Irene
blurted sharply. Immediately she wished she'd bitten her

tongue. There was no reason for so hostile a response nor for her to be suddenly feeling so defensive. She saw the questioning look on Sarah's face.

"Of course she could," Sarah replied, studying Irene more closely. "But it's comforting to me to know she has someone she can lean on."

Irene's frown returned. "Sometimes it can be damaging to lean on someone else too much."

Sympathy showed on Sarah's face. "I do recall that Jack was a bit overly protective of you."

An embarrassed flush reddened Irene's cheeks and a wave of guilt rushed through her. "Jack loved me and wanted to take care of me in every way. And I let him. It's my own fault I wasn't prepared for life after he was gone."

"But you've done very well on your own," Sarah said pointedly.

After I got past the panic, Irene added silently. Aloud, she said with pride, "Yes, Jeremy and I have done quite well."

Sarah grinned. "We Orman women all have spunk. We just have to find it sometimes."

Irene forced a smile. How had they gotten back to discussing her personal life? she wondered. That was the last thing she wanted to talk about. "Tell me about your trip to Australia," she requested, again changing the subject.

"Ah, the land down under," Sarah mused, showing no hesitation in a willingness to turn the conversation to herself and her travels. "It's so vast and with so many different kinds of environments. I honestly don't know where to start."

Listening to Sarah describe her trip, Irene began to relax. She drew a deep breath of the fresh night air and glanced up at the sky. Stars filled the heavens. She laughed as Sarah finished telling of a humorous encounter with a kangaroo.

Lazily her gaze traveled downward. Abruptly she stiffened. A figure, silhouetted by the lights from within, was visible on the upper balcony of the Brockman house. Murdock Parnell. She told herself to look away but instead her gaze remained fixed.

He was standing, leaning on the rail looking out over the water. As she watched, he straightened. In spite of the fact that he was no more than a shadow in the distance, she was sure he'd seen her and Sarah and was watching them. It was almost as if she could feel his gaze. Normally she would have waved. That was the neighborly thing to do. Instead the uneasiness she'd experienced earlier stirred within her. "I'm exhausted," she announced abruptly cutting into Sarah's story about a camping trip to the outback.

Sarah looked mildly surprised. Then glancing over the lake, she, too, saw the man on the balcony. "It would seem you haven't quite forgiven Mr. Parnell for scaring Jeremy," she remarked.

"I simply find the man a boor," Irene replied, scooting off the swing.

Sarah's expression became one of concern. "Is there something you're not telling me about Mr. Parnell's behavior? Was he crude? Offensive?"

"No," she admitted, recalling the genuine apology on his face. Unexpectedly she found herself thinking she'd never seen eyes quite so deep brown before. Quickly she shoved that thought from her mind. "He simply made it clear he was here for some privacy and solitude and I think we should respect his wishes," she added tersely.

"Of course, dear," Sarah agreed. But as she rose from her chair, she waved a greeting at the man on the balcony. "Just being neighborly," she said in response to Irene's impatient glance.

Irene saw the man give a short wave back. But she made no effort to follow her aunt's example. If she never had to see or speak to Mr. Parnell again before he left, she'd be happy.

Chapter Two

Murdock reeled in his line. The nightmares that had been haunting him for the past weeks had woken him in the small hours before dawn. Unwilling to return to them and feeling trapped within the confines of the house, he'd chosen to go fishing. His luck on the pier yesterday hadn't been good so he'd chosen to try a spot suggested by Horace. It was a small inlet near the far end of the lake. However, for over an hour now, he'd been sitting in Horace's rowboat, out on this icy lake and hadn't caught a thing more than four inches long. He frowned toward the jut of land that blocked his view of the main portion of the lake along with the caretaker's cabin. "Don't even think it," he ordered himself.

He cast his line in again. Nothing! The impatience on his face grew stronger. The beauty of this place should be enough to relax me, he told himself. He turned toward the east to see the sun beginning to break over the tops of the trees. Looks like one of those postcards you send to friends and they envy you for being in such a glorious environment, he thought. Still, his jaw refused to relax. Shifting his attention to the lake, he watched the fog moving over the surface of the water producing an eerie, almost surrealistic effect. But instead of enjoying nature's spectacle, he remained tense.

"In my book, getting chilled to the bone while not catching anything worth keeping qualifies as an emergency," he muttered under his breath.

Irene woke feeling restless. She knew she'd been dreaming. Vague images lingered in her mind. Jack was there and behind him was a tall, dark-haired man. It was Murdock Parnell. "How in the world did he get into my dreams," she grumbled, pushing the images out of her head as she rose from the bed. "He was probably the villain of the piece," she speculated as she headed for the bathroom. Firmly she told herself to forget him.

But a little later down in the kitchen, as she started the coffee, she found herself glancing out the window toward the Brockman house. Immediately she frowned at herself. Why she was even allowing Mr. Parnell a moment of her thoughts was a mystery.

She was just aware of him because, other than herself, Jeremy and Aunt Sarah, Mr. Parnell was the only other human being around for miles, she reasoned. With the exception of her home and the two acres that comprised her property, Horace Brockman owned all the rest of the land surrounding the lake and more. Her homestead was like a small island within the boundaries of his. In total he owned more than three hundred acres, all of which he'd left in its natural wooded state with the exception of a little more than an acre surrounding his home. "And caring for Horace's house and land is my responsibility. And that means that anyone staying there is sort of my responsibility too," she finished.

"Talking to yourself can be a sign you aren't getting out enough."

Irene turned to see Sarah entering the kitchen. "I get out plenty," she replied. "My seamstress work has been increasing steadily and, last school year, I worked part-time at Krindles Drugstore. I may do some waitressing at the café this year."

Sarah suddenly looked concerned. "Are you having financial difficulties?" she asked bluntly. "I thought you owned this house outright and Horace does pay you a decent salary to look after his property, doesn't he?"

"No, I'm not having financial difficulties," Irene assured her. "And, yes, I do own this house and Horace does pay me a decent salary to look after his property. I even have a little of Jack's insurance money left. But I've got to think of Jeremy's college education and I'd like a bit more of a cushion in case of an emergency."

Sarah continued to study her with concern. "I can understand your need to earn a little extra, but you should allow yourself some time for fun."

"Jeremy and I have plenty of fun. We fish and we go into town to a movie and out to dinner occasionally."

Sarah frowned impatiently. "I'll grant it's important for you and your son to spend time together but I was thinking of you spending a little more time with other adults and I don't mean in a work environment. It's not healthy for either him or you if your entire social life revolves around Jeremy."

"I promise I won't become an overly protective, overly possessive mother," Irene reassured her.

Sarah continued to frown. "You don't laugh like you used to."

"I've matured, that's all."

"There's a big difference between maturing and simply locking your feelings away."

The words to curtly tell her aunt that she wasn't locking her feelings inside formed on the tip of Irene's tongue but they refused to come out. She'd never been successful at lying to Sarah. "The coffee's ready. Would you like a cup?" she asked, letting her aunt know by the tone of her voice and the firm set of her jaw that this topic was now closed.

For a moment Sarah looked as if she was going to persist, then her expression softened and she said, "Yes, I'd love a cup."

Breathing a sigh of relief, Irene reached for a couple of mugs. But as she finished pouring the two cups of coffee, she glanced out the window once again and her back muscles stiffened.

The lake was large with several long fingerlike inlets hidden from her view. Coming out of one of those fingers at the far end of the lake was Horace's boat. Mr. Parnell had obviously been out on an early morning fishing expedition. She found herself hoping he'd been smart enough to dress warmly. A winter chill was already in the air and on the water the temperature would be even colder, especially before the sun had time to cast its warming rays.

I just don't want him getting sick and me having to call a doctor or, even worse, having to nurse him, she justified this unexpected rush of concern. Again ordering herself to put the man out of her mind, she carried her's and Sarah's coffee to the table. But as she began to sit down, she noticed that the sound of the motor on Horace's rowboat seemed to be getting closer. Walking over to the back door, she looked out and saw the boat heading toward her dock.

"It seems we're going to receive an early-morning call from the boorish Mr. Parnell," Aunt Sarah said, coming to stand beside Irene.

Irene looked up to see curiosity sparkling in Sarah's eyes. Her gaze swung back to the pier. Mr. Parnell had managed to moor the boat and was now climbing out. Normally she would have poured another cup of coffee and had it waiting for any guest who came in off the lake at this time of day, but the desire to get rid of Murdock Parnell as quickly as possible flowed through Irene. "I'll go see what he wants," she said, grabbing her coat and pulling it on as she strode out of the house.

Walking briskly, she managed to meet him halfway. "What can I do for you this morning, Mr. Parnell?" she asked bluntly.

"Please, call me Murdock," he requested.

She saw that he'd shoved his hands into his pockets and the red tint to his cheeks and nose verified that it had been cold on the water. She felt a little guilty not offering him the warmth of her house but every fiber of her being simply wanted to get rid of him as quickly as possible. "What can I do for you, Mr. Parnell?" she repeated in crisp business-like tones.

He frowned as if he found her determined anger toward him childish. Impatience entered his voice. "I'd like to speak to your husband."

She knew he had a right to be impatient with her. Normally she would not have remained angry with someone who had apologized as he had. Still, she chose to keep a chill between them. It was also obvious Horace had not told his guest that she was widowed and she found herself choosing not to relay this information, either. Instead she simply said, "He's not here."

The impatience on Murdock's face increased. "I didn't have much luck this morning fishing. Before I came here, Horace said I should try night crawlers for bait and that your husband could sell me some."

"My son, Jeremy, is the one who has worms to sell," she replied.

"You want to buy some worms?"

Irene jerked around at the sound of her son's voice to see both him and Sarah coming toward her and Murdock.

"Jeremy tells me you're Mr. Parnell," Sarah said, extending her hand toward Murdock.

"Please, call me Murdock," he requested with stiff politeness, obviously uncertain if her welcoming expression was genuine.

"I'm Irene's aunt Sarah," Sarah introduced herself as he accepted her offered handshake. When his hand closed around hers, she frowned. "You're freezing. Come on in and have a cup of coffee." She cast Irene a reproving glance. "I don't know what has happened to my niece's manners."

"I don't want to intrude," Murdock replied, with a pointed glance in Irene's direction to let her know he understood she did not want him in her home and he was perfectly willing to respect her wishes.

"It'll take me a few minutes to get the worms," Jeremy spoke up, looking worriedly at his mother as if afraid she would be angry with him for detaining the man.

Irene knew she was behaving badly. "My aunt's right," she admitted, forcing apology into her voice. "Please, come inside. I've just brewed a fresh pot of coffee."

For a moment Murdock hesitated and Irene was hopeful that he might stand by his refusal. Then he shrugged. "I could use something hot."

Sarah smiled brightly and slipped her arm through Murdock's. "How do you know Horace?" she asked as they started to the house.

"I work for him," Murdock replied.

Sarah regarded him with open curiosity. "I thought this place was Horace's hideaway. I'm sure Daisy told me he never allowed business associates to come here. In fact, he kept the place pretty much a secret."

"True," Murdock confirmed. He glanced over his shoulder at Jeremy who was walking alongside Irene. "How much for the worms?"

"Two dollars for a can full," the boy replied.

Murdock nodded his acceptance of the price and Jeremy turned and jogged toward the small storage barn a short distance from the house.

Clever diverting of the conversation, Irene thought. Clearly Murdock did not want to elaborate on why Horace had made an exception in his case. And I don't care why he's here, she assured herself. I'll just be happy when he leaves, she added. Still, she wondered if Sarah would persist in questioning the man.

As they entered the kitchen, Sarah went immediately to the cabinet and pulled out a mug and filled it. "Cream or sugar?" she asked.

Murdock had remained standing near the door. "Black," he answered.

"Irene makes pretty strong coffee," Sarah warned as she handed him the mug.

"I like it strong," he replied.

Irene had gone to the table and picked up the mug of coffee she'd poured for herself earlier. It was barely warm now but she chose to keep it. She did not however sit down. Instead she backed to the counter and stood watching Murdock. His presence seemed to fill the room and again the uneasiness she'd felt the day before stirred within her.

"We were just getting ready to fix breakfast," Sarah said, continuing to regard the man with interest. "Won't you join us?"

Irene felt like strangling her aunt at that moment. Somehow she managed to keep a polite expression on her face but she did not echo Sarah's invitation. Instead she remained silent, hoping Murdock would refuse.

"I really don't want to intrude," he replied.

Irene breathed a mental sigh of relief.

"Really, it's no bother. I was going to make parsley biscuits and scrambled eggs," Sarah said encouragingly.

If he does stay, his taste buds are in for a shock, Irene thought, recalling that Sarah always started with garlic and onions then added whatever suited her mood to her scrambled eggs. A dry grin tilted one side of her mouth. She wouldn't even be surprised if Sarah had started adding garlic to her biscuits.

"I appreciate the invitation," Murdock said, setting aside the coffee cup. "But I want to try my luck with the night crawlers."

Irene had seen him glance in her direction before he'd answered and knew he'd refused, at least partially, because of the lack of welcome in her expression. Feeling mildly guilty for being so inhospitable, she suddenly heard herself saying, "You should have a little something to eat." In the next moment, she was getting out a paper lunch bag and tossing in several of her homemade doughnuts. "I made these yesterday."

She saw the surprise in his eyes when she extended the bag to him. Well, he's not as surprised as I am, she thought.

For a moment she had the feeling he was going to refuse her offer. Then he reached out and accepted the bag. "Thanks," he said. "They smell good."

Irene barely managed a quick, "You're welcome." When his fingers had brushed against her hand she'd experienced a heat so intense it had caused a tingle to run up her arm. His hands are just extra warm from the coffee cup he's holding, she reasoned as she returned to her position by the counter. Still, she felt shaken.

"Your night crawlers are in the coffee can on the porch. They're good and big," Jeremy announced in businesslike tones as he entered the kitchen and crossed to the sink. "Mom won't let me bring them inside," he added as he washed his hands.

Irene breathed an under-her-breath sigh of relief. Jeremy's interruption was well-timed, she thought. And now Mr. Parnell would be leaving.

"Thanks." As he took a couple of dollars out of his wallet, Murdock's attention remained on the boy and his manner became that of one fisherman talking to another. "Horace told me there was a good fishing hole by the large boulder across the lake. You and your dad have any luck there?"

"My dad's dead," Jeremy replied matter-of-factly, as he dried his hands. "But mom and I have fished there and it's real good."

Murdock looked disconcerted and again Irene felt a rush of guilt.

"I'm sorry about your dad," Murdock said with sincerity, as he handed the boy the bills.

Jeremy gave a small shrug. "That's okay. He died a long time ago."

Irene saw accusation in Murdock's eyes as he glanced at her. He obviously felt very bad about having broached a subject that could have been painful to her son. "I supposed I should have mentioned I was widowed," she said stiffly.

Murdock's expression suddenly became apologetic. "It's none of my business." His gaze moved around the room, taking in the other occupants. "Thanks for your hospitality," he said and left.

His apology had held a note of sympathy and Irene felt even more like a heel. Well, I did give him some doughnuts she reminded herself.

"Good-looking man. Not as boyishly handsome as Jack was. There's a sort of ruggedness to his features but it gives him character, if you ask me. And he's polite, too," Sarah said.

Irene jerked her attention to her aunt to find Sarah regarding her with a thoughtful smile. Realizing she'd been staring at the door through which Murdock had exited, Irene frowned at herself. "I suppose he's not too hard on the eyes if a woman were interested in taking a second look, but I'm not." Determined to change the direction of this conversation, she added firmly, "Now how about breakfast? I'm starved."

"He's really not scary at all." Jeremy spoke up.

Irene turned to see her son looking out the back door. Moving so that she could follow his line of vision, she saw Murdock climb back into the rowboat and start the motor. He was wearing a bulky coat to protect against the icy morning breeze. Unexpectedly she found herself recalling how nicely built he looked beneath the heavy covering. Abruptly she turned away. The need to be busy was suddenly very strong. "How about pancakes instead of eggs and biscuits?" she suggested, striding to one of the cabinets and beginning to pull out the ingredients.

"Yes, pancakes," Jeremy seconded the suggestion.

"Pancakes sound good," Sarah agreed. "I can make my parsley biscuits for dinner."

Irene glanced over her shoulder at her son. He was still looking out the back door window. "Mr. Parnell is here for rest and relaxation. He doesn't want us disturbing him," she said, her voice carrying an order.

"Yes, ma'am," Jeremy replied, pulling his attention away from the lake.

"Talk about putting your foot in your mouth," Murdock muttered at himself as he guided the boat back across the lake. Of course it hadn't entirely been his fault. The woman could have mentioned that her husband was deceased when he'd first asked to speak to him.

Taking out one of the doughnuts he took a bite while he wondered why she hadn't. Maybe she thought he might try to make a pass at her if he knew she wasn't attached. Or maybe she found her husband's death still too painful to mention. Whichever it was, it didn't matter, he concluded. He just wished he'd never brought up the subject of her husband.

"Horace could have warned me," he grumbled. When Horace had given him instructions regarding the caretaker, Murdock had just assumed he was talking about a man.

"Here's the key and directions to my cabin," Horace had said. "Go there and rest a bit. You deserve it. There's a caretaker. Owns two acres on the lake across from my place. Damn nuisance I thought at first. I'd managed to buy up better than three hundred acres . . . all the rest of the land surrounding the lake and more. But the Galvins refused to sell. Turned out well, though. Honest, dependable people. I hired them to look after my place. Phone number's on the back of the map. Need anything including night crawlers, call them."

"I prefer to fish with flies," Murdock had managed to get in.

Horace smiled knowingly. "You go right ahead and try those fancy flies of yours but if you get serious and want to catch some really big fish, you go buy some night crawlers from Jeremy." Following this advice, Horace had launched into some fish stories and nothing more had been said about the Galvins.

"So now I know Jeremy is the son, Irene is the mother and Sarah is the mother's aunt," he repeated the names, to ensure he remembered them. The boy seemed like a good kid, he thought, and the aunt was interesting. The mother, however, was too defensive, too cold and clearly didn't like him. It would be best if he kept his distance in the future, he concluded.

"Good doughnuts, though," he admitted, taking out another.

"How's the fishing?"

The bright sun had warmed the day considerably. Murdock, half asleep, was sitting in a lawn chair on the pier with his line resting idly in the water. Jerking awake, he looked over his shoulder to find Jeremy Galvin standing on the bank behind him.

"Caught a couple of nice-size bass this morning with those worms you sold me," he said.

Jeremy smiled and moved tentatively to the beginning of the pier. "Mom and I always have good luck with them. 'Course I have to put hers on the hook for her. My grandpa Galvin showed me how."

Murdock straightened. Better be ready to guard my back, he mused dryly. "Your mom up at the house?" he asked.

"No." Jeremy shoved his hands into the pockets of his jeans and shifted from one foot to the other.

"You're not supposed to be here, right?" Murdock guessed, bracing himself for another confrontation with the she-bear from across the lake.

Jeremy grinned sheepishly. "I'm not really disobeying. My mom had to go over to Mrs. Kolinski's house. Mom's doing some sewing for her." An expression of distaste came onto his face. "Usually, when she has to go somewhere on a Saturday, I have to go with her 'cause I'm not in school and she won't let me stay at home alone yet. But since Aunt Sarah's here visiting, Mom let me stay with her. And Aunt Sarah said I could go for a walk as long as I didn't go far, stayed on our private road here and didn't go out on the main road and didn't go wandering off into the woods. This isn't far, I'm practically on the road and I'm not wandering in the woods. Besides, Mom lets me come over here and fish when the Brockmans aren't here."

Recalling the many times in his youth he'd stretched his parents' orders to the limit, Murdock grinned. "Sounds like you're here legally."

Uncertainty suddenly shadowed Jeremy's face. "If you really want to be left alone, I'll leave."

Murdock reminded himself he had come here seeking solitude but the wistful look on the boy's face touched a chord deep within him. "Guess it's a little tough on a guy living with only women," he said.

"My grandpa Galvin comes and takes me fishing sometimes. And last summer I got to go to Alaska and stay with my grandpa and grandma Orman and grandpa Orman took me camping, and we got to see some seals and caribou. And my mom is real good about doing stuff with me. We go fishing and she's good at playing catch." He paused to grimace self-consciously. "But, yeah, sometimes it can be hard on a guy when there's only women around."

Murdock couldn't stop himself from smiling. "I don't mind a little company."

Jeremy grinned and quickly walked down the pier and seated himself cross-legged, Indian fashion, a little away from Murdock's chair. "What do you do?" he asked. "For a job, I mean."

"I design and install computer systems." Images he'd come here to forget suddenly flooded Murdock's mind. They were the core of his nightmares. He shoved them back into the dark recesses.

"My mom has a computer. Mr. Brockman gave it to her to keep the accounts. He said that because he was in the computer business he felt his caretaker should use one. He even paid for her to take classes on how to use it. And he sent me some games to play on it. He told my mom that computers were the tools of today and the future and I should get used to using one." Jeremy's eyes glistened. "I'm pretty good, too."

"Good marketing ploy," Murdock said with a laugh. "Hook 'em while they're young."

Jeremy smiled lopsidedly as if he didn't quite understand the joke but was too proud to ask. Then his gaze shifted across the lake. "Aunt Sarah's going to cook dinner."

Murdock heard the dubious note in his voice. "She's not such a good cook, uh?"

"Well." Jeremy screwed up his mouth into an exaggerated look of thoughtfulness. "My mom calls Aunt Sarah's meals an adventure. They usually taste pretty good, actually. They're just a bit strange sometimes and you have to like onions and garlic. Aunt Sarah says those are good for your blood and she uses them in nearly everything."

"Apparently she's fond of parsley, too," Murdock said, recalling Sarah saying something about making parsley biscuits.

"That, too," Jeremy conceded. "She likes to use all kinds of stuff. She made brownies with jalapeño peppers once."

Murdock grimaced. "She sounds a little dangerous around a stove."

"They weren't that bad," Jeremy admitted in his aunt's defense. "But they weren't that good, either," he added honestly. His gaze shifted to the water, then back to Murdock. "My dad was a lineman for the telephone company."

Surprised by this sudden change in subject, Murdock wasn't certain what to say. "I've heard that's a tough job" was all he could come up with.

"He got killed during a storm. I was barely four at the time. I sort of don't remember him very well anymore."

Murdock hid his surprise that Irene Galvin had been widowed so long. Her defensiveness had caused him to believe she'd lost her husband more recently. Again uncertain of how to respond, he said, "I think it's only natural for your memories to grow dim after a period of time."

Jeremy nodded. "Great-aunt Sarah says you have to bury your dead. She says it's nice to remember the good times but a person has to get on with their life." Jeremy frowned. "I think she's worried about my mom."

"Your mother seems like a woman who can take care of herself," Murdock said encouragingly.

"What's a cynic?" Jeremy asked abruptly.

The child's shifts in conversation were difficult to follow, Murdock thought, again taken unawares. "A cynic," he said slowly, stalling for time to think. "I always think of a cynic as someone who is critical of everything. Someone who dwells on the bad instead of the good in things."

Jeremy frowned. "Aunt Sarah is wrong. My mom's not like that."

Now Murdock frowned. "Your aunt Sarah told you your mom is a cynic?"

"No," Jeremy said quickly. "I heard them, Mom and Aunt Sarah, talking last night out on the porch." A flash of guilt again showed on his face. "I wasn't really eavesdropping. I was in bed and I had my window open a little. So, I just heard them. They weren't arguing. Aunt Sarah was just saying she thought my mom should date and my mom told her she was happy with her life just the way it is."

Murdock recalled the chill he'd seen in Irene Galvin's eyes. He couldn't imagine any man wanting to face that over a candlelight dinner. "I'm sure your mom knows what's best for her."

"Yeah," Jeremy replied with an emphatic nod. In the next instant, his assurance faltered. "It's just that every once in a while she looks so sad."

"No one's happy a hundred percent of the time," Murdock said pointedly, trying to picture the cool Mrs. Galvin with even a hint of warmth on her face, and failing. "Your mom's one tough lady. I'm sure she'll do just fine on her own."

Jeremy smiled with relief. "That's what she says."

And that describes her to a *T,* Murdock thought.

The sound of metal clanging suddenly filled the air. Jeremy twisted to look across the lake. "Uh, oh! Mom's home," he said.

Following the boy's line of vision, Murdock could make out a jeans-clad figure on the porch of the Galvin home. This morning he'd noticed a metal triangle like the one used in Western movies to summon the wranglers to dinner, hanging near the back door. That, he realized, was what had been rung. He saw the woman looking his way but, like last night, he noted, she didn't wave. Instead she stood with her arms akimbo.

Jeremy scrambled to his feet. "I'd better be going."

"Since she's already seen you here, you might as well let me give you a ride home in the boat. That'll be faster," Murdock offered. Inwardly he frowned at himself. He'd come here to relax, not face the wrath of a disobeyed mother. But he felt protective toward the boy. *I'm just trying to make up for scaring him the first time we met,* he told himself as he began reeling in his line.

Jeremy regarded him uncertainly. "I don't want to be a bother. I can walk home."

"It's no bother," Murdock assured him.

"It might be best if you don't tell her we were talking about her," Jeremy suggested.

"I was thinking the same thing myself," Murdock agreed, setting his rod aside and handing the boy a life jacket.

Looking relieved, Jeremy climbed into the boat. But as they headed out across the lake, Murdock noticed the relief vanish and the child's expression become one of someone prepared to take his medicine.

Irene watched the boat nearing her pier. Jeremy was usually very good about obeying her. She didn't understand why he'd gone over to see Murdock Parnell. As the boat reached the dock, Jeremy tossed her the rope and she secured it around a post. "I hope Jeremy hasn't been making a nuisance of himself," she said with stiff apology when Murdock cut off the motor. Her gaze shifted to her son and her tone became reprimanding. "Sarah said she's been keeping an eye on you and you've been sitting on Mr. Brockman's pier for quite a while."

"He wasn't being a nuisance," Murdock spoke up. "We were just exchanging some guy talk."

Surprised by the man's quick defense of her son, Irene glanced at him. There was a protectiveness in his eyes that shook her. Quickly she turned back to her son. "Guy talk?"

she asked to cover the sudden disconcertedness she was feeling.

Jeremy's shoulders straightened with masculine pride. "Yeah, you know. You women have your women talk and we men have our guy talk . . . fishing, stuff like that."

He looked like such a little adult, Irene couldn't stop herself from smiling. "Well, I think it's time for you to come visit with your great-aunt Sarah for a while. She's been making cookies."

Jeremy eyed his mother dubiously. "What kind of cookies?"

"She said something about pumpkin and cranberry, I think." Irene gave him an encouraging look. "They smell real good."

"Another adventure," Jeremy said, knowingly. He turned back to Murdock with an impish grin. "Would you like a cookie?"

"Think I'll skip it this time," Murdock replied, giving him a comradely wink.

Irene was forced to admit that at that moment, Murdock Parnell looked appealing. The admission made her tense. Remembering her manners, she said politely, "Thank you for bringing my son home."

Murdock turned his attention to her. "You're welcome."

As their gazes momentarily locked, she experienced an unexpected urge to encourage him to come to the house. Shaken by her reactions to this man, the need to escape his company became overwhelming. "Good day, Mr. Parnell," she said with dismissal, and headed toward the house leaving Jeremy to untie the boat.

"I don't understand why you're still angry with Mr. Parnell," Jeremy said, catching up with her on the porch. "He's really real nice."

Irene frowned at herself. She knew she'd overreacted and she had sounded decidedly inhospitable again. "I'm not angry with Mr. Parnell," she confessed with a tired sigh. "He just makes me nervous."

Jeremy looked at her in confusion. "Why?"

"I'd like to know the answer to that myself," Sarah interjected from the kitchen door. "He seems like a polite, pleasant man to me."

"He just makes me uneasy, that's all," Irene replied.

"Could it be that you find him attractive and that threatens this determined isolationism you've imposed on yourself?" Sarah asked.

Jeremy looked confused. "Why would Mom act angry if she really liked him?"

"Because she's determined to be vinegar rather than honey when it comes to trying to attract bees," Sarah replied.

The confusion on Jeremy's face grew stronger. "Huh?"

"Never mind your great-aunt Sarah," Irene told him. Her gaze shifting from her son to her aunt, she continued, "I do not find Mr. Parnell attractive, therefore, I don't feel threatened by him. I am also not angry with him. The fact is, I don't feel anything about him either way. Now I'd like to drop the subject and try one of those cookies you've been baking."

Jeremy looked at her as if her desire for one of Sarah's cookies was causing him to question her sanity but he remained silent.

"Only a fool lies to herself," Sarah said stepping aside to allow Irene and Jeremy to enter.

"I know what I want and getting married again isn't it," Irene snapped back. "I like my life just as it is."

Sarah gave her a hug. "I'm sorry. You've said that enough I should believe you. All I want is for you to be happy." Releasing her, she picked up a freshly baked cookie. "Try this."

"Mom?"

Irene looked down to see Jeremy watching her worriedly.

"Everything is fine," she assured him. Picking up another cookie, she handed it to him. "We'll do this together," she said, positioning her cookie in front of her mouth and giving him a look to let him know she expected him to do the same. "We take a bite on the count of three."

Sarah shook her head. "You two are a trial." Then as they took their bites and ate them, she grinned. "Good, aren't they."

"Different." Irene qualified her answer. "But the taste sort of grows on you."

"Not on me," Jeremy confessed, setting aside the remainder of his cookie. "Guess maybe it's an adult taste."

"Maybe Mr. Parnell might like a few," Sarah suggested.

Jeremy looked horrified. "I don't think so," he said quickly.

Her son's attempt to protect the man from Sarah's experiment caused Irene to realize just how fond Jeremy was growing of the man. Again her nerves tensed. Her son could be persistent when he chose and she wasn't looking forward to having Mr. Parnell showing up at her dock on a regular basis. He's only going to be here for a short while, she reminded herself. He'd be leaving soon and that would be the end of him.

As Murdock guided the boat away from the dock, he glanced over his shoulder to see Irene Galvin striding to her house with her son jogging to catch up with her. His attention caught by the seductive swing of her hips, he found himself again thinking that she had nice curves. And she had looked kind of cute when she'd smiled, he added.

"And this altitude is affecting my brain," he muttered under his breath. She might be widowed but she hadn't buried her husband. Even more, she'd clearly placed Murdock at the top of her "people I don't like" list. "She's a cold, stubborn woman who makes snap judgments about people and refuses to admit she could have made a mistake." He'd never had any patience with people like that and why she was still on his mind was a mystery to him.

Chapter Three

Irene stood on the doorstep of the Brockman house. She'd waited until after dinner when Jeremy was teaching Sarah how to play one of his computer games, then she'd excused herself saying she wanted to go for a walk. After bidding goodbye to Murdock Parnell today on her dock, she'd hoped that would be the last she would see of him until Monday when she had to come to clean. But here she was seeking him out. She raised her hand to knock, then hesitated. Maybe this wasn't necessary, she told herself.

You're afraid to face him, her inner voice taunted her. I'm not afraid of any man, she returned and knocked firmly.

Surprise registered on Murdock's face when he opened the door.

"I was wondering if I could have a few moments of your time." Silently she berated herself. During her walk here, she'd practiced saying this with cool politeness, instead it had come out harshly.

Murdock scowled. "If you've come to tell me to stay away from your son, I'd like to point out that he was the one who sought me out."

This is going to be embarrassing, Irene groaned mentally. "That's not exactly why I'm here." The worry she'd been trying to hide suddenly showed on her face.

Curiosity entered Murdock's eyes. "Would you like to come in?"

She nodded and as he stepped aside, she entered. Normally she was comfortable in this house. But even with a fire burning in the fireplace giving the room a cheery warmth, she remained ill at ease.

"Would you like to sit down?" Murdock offered. "I have some coffee made."

Irene had been staring at the fire. Turning to him she suddenly found herself wondering what it would be like to sit next to him and watch the flames dancing on the logs. Her mind flashed back to nights spent that way with Jack. Her stomach knotted. The need to finish her business and escape was powerful. "No, thank you," she replied, forcing a calmness into her voice. Her gaze had fallen on his arms. He'd rolled his shirtsleeves up to just below the elbow and she saw a bandage wrapped around his left arm just above the wrist and the lower portion of his right arm was sporting a large bruise. A concern for him swept through her.

"I was in an accident," he said, noticing the direction of her gaze.

"If you need the bandage redone, my aunt's a nurse," she heard herself offering.

"Thanks, I'll keep that in mind. But I doubt I'll need her services. The wound's pretty well healed."

She heard the cool edge in his voice as if he didn't quite believe her solicitous attitude and knew she deserved it. She hadn't been particularly friendly and a part of her wanted to apologize for her standoffishness. But another part felt safer with this chilly shield between them. Just ask him what you came to ask and get out of here, she ordered herself. "I was wondering what you and Jeremy talked about."

He raised an eyebrow. "Are you worried I might be a bad influence on your son?"

"No," she replied honestly. "Horace likes you and I trust his judgment. Besides, I've talked to Jeremy about what's proper behavior and what is not." Her expression hardened to cover her self-consciousness. "And I questioned him about his conversation with you. He said talking to you was like talking to his grandfather."

"I suppose I should be relieved to hear that," Murdock returned dryly. "I'm not interested in having the local sheriff on my doorstep." Abruptly his expression softened. "I shouldn't have sounded so harsh. You're right to have questioned him. A parent should be careful about strangers."

She'd half expected him to throw her out. Instead there was approval in his voice. A warm glow of pleasure threatened to spread through her. She hadn't come here to learn to like the man, she reminded herself. Extinguishing the spreading warmth, she returned her full attention to the purpose that had brought her here. "While I am satisfied that you are not a bad influence on my son," she said stiffly, "I am still concerned about his reason for seeking you out. I need to know if he's worried or troubled by something he feels he needs another 'guy' to talk to about."

"No. Like he said, we were just talking about 'stuff.' Nothing earth-shattering. You women have your gossip sessions and we men have our little talks."

"What a wonderfully chauvinistic observation," she returned.

A mischievous gleam sparkled in his eyes. "This wilderness atmosphere does seem to bring out the macho instincts in me."

Irene's breath locked in her lungs. With that playful look in his eyes and that hint of a smile at the corner of his mouth, he looked unbelievably appealing. She found herself wondering how it would feel if he kissed her. Something very akin to panic swept through her. She didn't want to be attracted to him or to any man. She backed toward the door. "I really should be leaving." With her hand on the knob, she added, "Have a good evening," and in the next instant she was outside on the porch, closing the door behind her. Realizing her hands were shaking, she shoved them into the pockets of her jacket. "I can't believe I actually wondered what it would feel like to have him kiss me," she murmured under her breath. "I don't even really know the man."

She took a deep calming breath. "I'm sure it was just a momentary lapse of sanity." Her jaw firmed. "It won't happen again."

Murdock stood frowning at the door through which Irene Galvin had fled. And she had fled. That was the only word to describe her abrupt exit. He'd also noticed the momentary glint of feminine interest in her eyes and the flash of heat in those blue depths had startled him.

Clearly she wasn't the ice maiden he'd begun to believe she was. But her quick escape also let him know she had no intention of giving in to this warmer side of her nature. "If she wants to stay an iceberg, that's just fine with me," he informed the door. He glanced toward the fireplace. The fire was burning cheerfully, inviting him back. Instead, his gaze returned to the door. He hadn't heard a car. That meant she was on foot. Abruptly he strode to the fireplace and closed the glass front. Assured the house was safe, he grabbed his coat from the peg by the door, the flashlight from the shelf above and hurried outside.

"My mother taught me that it was only polite to walk a woman home."

Irene jerked around to see Murdock approaching at a fast clip. Silhouetted in the moonlight, he looked even more imposing than she remembered. The thought that if a woman wanted to be protected, he was the man who could do it played through her mind. But she didn't need anyone other than herself to protect her, her inner voice retorted curtly. "There is really no need," she said as he reached her. "I've walked this road hundreds, probably thousands of times. I know it like the back of my hand."

"That wouldn't make any difference to my mother," he replied.

The firmness in his voice let her know arguing would be useless. "Obviously this wilderness atmosphere also brings out the chivalry in you," she remarked dryly, again beginning to walk toward her home.

"Obviously," he replied, falling into step beside her.

A terse silence hung between them and she knew she'd behaved badly. "It's really rather nice of you to see me home," she admitted stiffly. "I just don't want you to feel obligated if there is anything else you'd rather be doing."

"The truth is I was enjoying the fire," he replied honestly. "However, this is a beautiful night for a walk. And I prefer being outside to being inside."

She caught a subtle edge in his voice when he made this last admission that caused her to glance at him. She could have sworn she saw a hauntedness momentarily cloud his features. But then it could have merely been the play of shadows caused by the luminous but eerie glow of the full moon, she told herself, as he turned to her with an expression of impersonal politeness.

"I was also thinking of buying another can of night crawlers from Jeremy for tomorrow morning," he said.

His demeanor and tone were letting her know there was absolutely nothing personal about him walking her home. As he returned his attention to the road, she experienced a tiny jab deep within. It felt almost like a touch of disappointment. But it's not, she assured herself. "Jeremy will appreciate the business," she returned in an equally indifferent voice.

"He seems like a good kid," Murdock opined.

"He is," she replied.

Having expended their topics of mutual interest, a silence fell between them. Irene attempted to ignore the man walking beside her but instead his presence caused her muscles to tense and the stillness between them only served to increase her awareness of him. "Nice weather we've been having, although we could use some rain," she said, hoping conversation would be a distraction.

"Yeah," he replied.

His monosyllabic response gave her the distinct impression he wasn't interested in talking. Deciding that forcing him wasn't going to help ease her tension she said no more. Instead she attempted to focus her attention on the sounds of the night and the road in front of them.

They'd gone a short distance more when Murdock asked, "Have you lived here long?"

Surprised by this unexpected burst of dialogue, she glanced at him. There was a tense set to his jaw and she had the impression he was seeking a diversion from whatever had been on his mind. "Ten years," she replied. Admitting that her attempt to concentrate on anything other than him had not been entirely successful, she chose to try to keep this conversation going. "My husband bought the place a few months before we were married. We both grew up in Alexandria."

"That isn't too far from here, is it? Maybe a two-hour drive?" he asked.

"Something like that," she replied. "When Jack was just a kid, his grandpa used to bring him to this lake on overnight camping trips. Jack always swore that one day, he'd have a home here." Abruptly she stopped herself. Talking about Jack wasn't difficult anymore. She'd dealt with her grief. Her time with Jack was like a packet of memories tied in a pretty pink bow. Most were pleasant, some were bittersweet but she could handle them. However, she was sure Murdock Parnell didn't really want to hear about her and Jack. Think of another topic, she ordered herself, as a fresh silence began to fall between them. But making small talk wasn't her forte.

As she grappled for a subject, Murdock suddenly said, "Isn't it a little isolated out here for a woman alone?"

Irene was surprised by the depth of concern in his voice. The man is definitely the male protector type, she noted, a warning signal going off in her brain. Her determination to keep her distance grew stronger. "Not for me. I'm used to it. Besides, we're less than fifteen minutes from Hares Burrow and barely twenty minutes from Pine River. And if I get real lonely or need help, nearly all of Jack's family still lives in and around Alexandria. I can run down there for the weekend."

"Sounds like you've got your life orchestrated well," Murdock observed.

"It suits me," she replied firmly.

They had reached her home and she drew a mental breath of relief. She turned to thank him and say good-night when she recalled that he'd said he wanted more night crawlers.

She was considering getting them herself when the door was suddenly opened.

"Murdock, how nice to see you again," Sarah said with a welcoming smile. Her gaze shifted from him to her niece.

"I needed to speak to Mr. Parnell and he walked back with me because he wants to buy some night crawlers from Jeremy," Irene said quickly, not wanting her aunt to get the wrong impression.

"Then he should come in from the cold," Sarah insisted, waving them both inside.

Jeremy poked his head around from behind Sarah. "I'll go get the worms." In the next instant he was on his way to the back door.

Feeling swept along, Irene mounted the porch with Murdock following.

"Let me take your coat," Sarah offered, as Murdock stepped into the house.

"I won't be staying long. I'll just keep it on," he replied.

Irene again experienced a sense of relief. The way his presence seemed to fill her home unnerved her. Mentally she chided herself for behaving cowardly, but the impulse to put distance between him and her was too strong to resist. "I'm going to hang my coat up," she said, heading to the kitchen. Once there, she planned to hide out until he left.

But as she started down the hall, she heard Sarah say, "We'll just go along with Irene. You must try my cookies."

Glancing over her shoulder, she saw Sarah hooking her arm through Murdock's. Silently she groaned as they followed her into the kitchen.

I'm just not used to having unattached men in my home, she reasoned as she slipped off her coat and hung it on the peg by the back door. Then she was forced to recall that Don Loggen had been by just last week with firewood. He'd even flirted with her and tried to get her to go out with him. And, just two weeks ago Buck Hastings had come calling and sat on her porch and eaten apple pie. In both cases, she'd had no trouble remaining indifferent to their company.

A prickling at the back of her neck caused her to glance over her shoulder. Out of the corner of her eye, she caught a glimpse of Murdock watching her before he quickly turned his attention to Sarah. That she'd actually been able to feel his gaze on her caused her already taut nerves to tense even further.

"The pumpkin and cranberry tastes blend a lot better than I thought they would," Murdock was saying as Irene turned fully around.

Continuing to stand near the back door, she watched him take another large bite.

Sarah beamed. "I'll just pack some up for you," she said, already searching for a bag to put them in. When it looked as if he was going to protest, she held her hand up. "I insist."

Murdock gave a single shoulder shrug and took another bite.

Irene had to admit her aunt's cookies had an interesting taste but she was surprised he seemed to like them so much. The thought that his own cooking might be really bad and he might merely be so hungry he was willing to eat anything, crossed her mind. "Would you like some fried chicken? We had some left over from dinner," she heard herself offering.

There was surprise on his face when he turned to her. "No, thanks. I broiled a steak and baked a potato for dinner."

His self-reliant air let her know he was perfectly capable of feeding himself and she wished she'd bitten her tongue. She also wished he'd look away. He was studying her as if she was a oddity he found difficult to understand and the muscles in her back tightened to the point they felt like violin strings. "That's nice," she managed to say stiffly.

"Are you married?" Sarah asked, approaching Murdock and extending the bag of cookies.

As his gaze turned to her aunt, one part of Irene was grateful to Sarah for diverting his attention while another part was mortified. Murdock Parnell's marital state was none of their business.

"No," he replied in an easy drawl.

Sarah continued to study him. "Are you here getting over a divorce or a relationship that went sour?"

Irene wanted to crawl into a hole. What had gotten into her aunt? she wondered. Sarah was naturally blunt but she usually didn't pry into strangers lives so crassly. "Really, Aunt Sarah," she gasped, then she saw the amused gleam in Murdock's eyes.

"Neither," he answered Sarah's question in the same easy drawl.

Sarah nodded her approval. "Seeings how Jeremy seems to be seeking out your company, I just thought I should make sure you weren't going to try to turn him against women."

Irene breathed a mental sigh of relief. What had looked like a flagrant act of matchmaking now appeared to be merely a great-aunt's concern for her great-nephew.

"I'm harboring no grudges," Murdock told Sarah. "I like women."

The masculine appreciation of the female gender evident in his voice caused a curl of excitement deep within Irene. Immediately she fought against this unwanted reaction. Then he glanced toward her. The cool indifference in his eyes let her know she wasn't one of the women he found appealing. With no further effort on her part, the excitement turned to a chill. She assured herself she was glad he wasn't interested in her. But she didn't feel glad. Instead she experienced the sharp sting of having been insulted.

For some reason her hormones were obviously overreacting today, she decided. But by tomorrow, she vowed, she would make certain they were back to normal.

Jeremy came in at that moment and announced that the can of worms was on the back porch.

Thank goodness, Irene sighed silently. Now Murdock could be on his way. And he was more than happy to be leaving she noted as he quickly thanked Sarah for the cookies, paid the boy and headed to the door. But when he reached for the knob, Irene heard herself saying, "Would you like me to give you a ride back to the Brockmans' place?"

Mentally she gasped as her words echoed in her mind. She couldn't believe she'd said that. Hadn't she wanted to be rid of him? Offering him a ride was the neighborly thing to do and she'd always tried to be a good neighbor, she reminded herself.

For a moment he hesitated as if actually considering the offer, then he shook his head. "No, thanks. It's a nice night and I enjoy walking."

Again Irene experienced the slap of insult. She was certain that had she been anyone else he would have accepted the ride. Well, I'm glad he didn't, she told herself as the door closed behind him. Now she wouldn't have to try to think of some mundane thing to say to pass the time while she drove him home. "Well, you certainly charmed Mr. Parnell," Sarah observed dourly.

Irene turned to see her aunt regarding her reprovingly. "I wasn't trying to charm him."

Sarah shook her head. "If I was a few years younger, I'd at least want to take a closer look before I wrote him off."

"I was under the impression age wasn't supposed to matter anymore," Irene returned, her tone implying that as far as she was concerned her aunt was free to pursue Mr. Parnell.

Sarah's mouth formed a thoughtful pout. "You're right," she conceded. Then she breathed a sigh. "But as attractive as I find him, there's no spark."

"Sparks aren't flying around me, either," Irene asserted.

"Sparks?" Jeremy asked, looking from one woman to the other in confusion.

"Allurement, fascination, attraction, animal magnetism," Sarah elaborated.

Jeremy scowled at them. "Well, I think he's nice."

"And so do we," Sarah reassured him. "Very nice," she added, giving Irene a hard look.

"He's nice," Irene agreed to keep the peace. But recalling the cool gaze he'd turned on her, she was sure he wouldn't have used that adjective to describe her. And I'm glad, she told herself. Picking up a cookie on her way, she headed into the living room to read the paper.

But after only a few minutes, she set the paper aside. "Those cookies kind of grow on you," she said, rising from the couch and heading back into the kitchen. As she stood by the table reaching for another cookie, she knew this had been an excuse to escape from the others. Grabbing her coat off the hook to ward off the chilly night air, she stepped out onto the back porch.

There she stood watching the Brockman house. "I'm just worried about him getting home safely. There are bears and other wild animals around and he is sort of my responsibility," she grumbled under her breath, angry with herself for not having been able to put Murdock Parnell out of her mind.

She glanced at her watch. He'd left a little over ten minutes ago. The road had to weave around one of the coves in the lake making the distance by land between her house and the Brockman's about a mile. Walking at a brisk pace, he should be reaching the house soon, she judged.

As the next minutes passed slowly, a chill unrelated to the wind caused her to shiver. The worry that something might have happened to him pervaded her. He looks like a man who can take care of himself, she argued.

His image suddenly filled her mind. He definitely looked like a man who could take care of himself, she reaffirmed. A wave of feminine approval brought a rush of heat. Scowling at herself, she drew in a deep breath of the cold night air. The embers his image had begun to bring to life smoldered. Still, in spite of his remembered physical strength, her anxiousness remained.

It's my fault he's out there tonight. That's the only reason I'm so concerned, she told herself.

In the house across the lake she thought she saw some movement. Then a man's form filled one of the sections of the glass doors that led out to the lower deck from the living room.

Drawing a relieved breath, she turned to go inside. A gasp of surprise escaped. Sarah was standing just outside the door, watching her. The realization that she'd been so intent on Murdock Parnell she hadn't even heard her aunt step outside shook her.

"Looks like he made it home just fine," Sarah remarked, continuing to study Irene with interest.

"I felt responsible for him," she replied defensively. Her jaw firmed. "And that's all."

"If you say so," Sarah returned, but she didn't look convinced.

Irene's jaw firmed even more. "I do say so." Brushing past her aunt she went inside.

"Actually I came looking for you to tell you I've discovered who our Mr. Parnell is," Sarah said, following her inside.

Irene caught the edge of excitement in Sarah's voice. As she hung her coat on the peg, she glanced over her shoulder at her aunt. "What do you mean by 'who our Mr. Parnell is'?"

Sarah paused to hang her own wrap on a peg, then picked up a magazine lying on a nearby counter. "He's in here." She smiled broadly. "He's a hero."

"A hero?" Irene echoed, the words causing her stomach to knot.

"It's all in here." Sarah brandished the magazine in front of her. "The article doesn't identify him by name. It only says he's an American computer expert who was installing a system in a bank in Chile when that earthquake hit. But that's him in this picture."

Irene looked at the picture her aunt was thrusting in front of her. In it a man was emerging from a badly damaged building with a child in one arm and half carrying, half dragging a woman in the other. They were dirty and bloodied and their expressions strained from the terror they had just lived through but Irene knew without a doubt that the man was Murdock Parnell. "All right, I'll admit, it's him," she said.

"The major portion of the building he was in collapsed," Sarah continued triumphantly. "According to bank customers and workers, he saved the lives of two women and a child."

Irene recalled the injuries on Murdock's arms and her stomach knotted even more tightly. "Lucky for them he was there. That also explains why Horace broke his rule and allowed one of his employees to use his hideaway."

Sarah nodded. "And I think we should invite Murdock over tomorrow for Sunday dinner. He certainly deserves a good home-cooked meal."

"No." The word burst forth before Irene could stop it. Surprise registered on Sarah's face and Irene wished she'd been less blunt. Feeling the need to explain, she said stiffly, "I've had my fill of heroes. Jack was the hero type...always the first one out when a storm hit . . . always the first one up the pole."

An embarrassed flush darkened Irene's cheeks. "I didn't mean that the way it sounded," she continued hurriedly. "I know the world needs heroes. I was proud of Jack. The problem was with me. I thought he'd always be here. I didn't expect to be widowed at twenty-four with a child to raise on my own."

Irene clamped her mouth shut. She couldn't believe she'd spoken these thoughts aloud. Until now she'd held them shut tightly inside. "I know that sounds selfish and immature," she said stiffly.

"It sounds human," Sarah replied, moving to her and giving her a hug. Releasing her niece, Sarah studied Irene worriedly. "It also sounds as if you haven't fully dealt with Jack's death."

Irene met her aunt's gaze steadily. "Yes, I have. I cried out the pain of losing him and I've talked to my mother, my mother-in-law, you and others about my feelings of loss. I've accepted my widowhood and I'm getting on with my life."

"You've talked about how sad it was for Jack to have been taken from us at so young an age and you've admitted to missing him." Sarah's expression became stern. "Those are platitudes. Maybe it's time you talked about how you really felt.''

''That was how I really felt,'' Irene returned.

Sarah raised a disbelieving eyebrow.

Her self-restraint already stretched to the breaking point by her reactions to Murdock, old pain and anger she'd worked hard for years to suppress bubbled to the surface and tore at Irene. The tenuous control she was exercising over her emotions snapped. ''All right! So I also felt angry and deserted, too,'' she confessed. Guilt assailed her. ''I knew Jack hadn't wanted to die. But that didn't change the fact that he had and he'd left me on my own after promising to be with me until we were old and gray.''

Irene paced the room. ''Maybe it wasn't even anger so much as fear. I wasn't really sure I could make it on my own without him.''

''But you did,'' Sarah noted.

Irene's shoulders squared with pride. ''Yes, I did.'' Her gaze leveled pointedly on her aunt. ''And I'm happy with my life just the way it is.''

Sarah regarded her skeptically. ''So you keep saying.'' A challenge entered her eyes. ''However, if that's really the case, why are you behaving as if Murdock Parnell is a threat?''

Irene frowned. ''He's not a threat.''

''Then why shouldn't we invite him to dinner?'' Sarah argued. ''It's the neighborly thing to do.''

''Because after your barrage of questions, he's bound to think you're matchmaking,'' Irene returned.

Sarah grinned. ''Well, if he does and he still comes that could prove interesting.''

Again Murdock's image filled Irene's mind. And for a moment she was tempted, then the protective wall she was determined to maintain around herself again grew strong. "No," she said firmly.

Sarah frowned with impatience. "You need to spend some time with marriageable men. If you don't, when Mr. Right comes along, you won't even know how to behave to lure him in."

Irene met Sarah's look of impatience with one of her own. "I met and married my Mr. Right. I don't want nor expect to find another."

"You can be downright stubborn when you've set your mind to something," Sarah complained. She breathed a frustrated sigh. "Someday you may be sorry you didn't take my advice. Jeremy won't be here forever. One day he'll go off on his own and then you'll be all alone."

"You've managed just fine on your own," Irene observed.

"Yes, and I'll agree it's better to be on your own than to marry simply to have another person around," Sarah replied. "But I'd never pass up the opportunity to find someone I would enjoy sharing my life with."

Irene recalled that instant when she'd actually wondered what it would feel like to be kissed by Murdock Parnell. You're asking for trouble if you let down your guard, her inner voice warned and she vanquished the memory. "Right now all I want is to go to bed and get some sleep," she said. "And tomorrow we'll have a family day. Just you, me and Jeremy. We don't get to see you very often and I think the three of us should spend some time together."

"I suppose I should be flattered and I do love spending time with only you and Jeremy," Sarah admitted. A mischievous gleam suddenly sparkled in her eyes. "But I do enjoy having a handsome, virile male around, too. It sort of adds a bit of excitement to the atmosphere."

Irene couldn't stop herself from smiling. "You are much more incorrigible than I ever would have believed," she said, giving her aunt a hug. "But let's allow Mr. Parnell to have his solitude." Mischievousness suddenly showed in her eyes as well. "However, if you should spot anyone in church tomorrow you think *you* might be interested in pursuing, just let me know. I'll be happy to invite them to dinner."

"I'll take you up on that," Sarah promised with a grin.

Chapter Four

As Irene entered the church the next morning and followed Jeremy into their usual spot in the last pew to the left of the aisle, she again felt in total charge of her world. Sarah had not once mentioned Mr. Parnell this morning and Irene was convinced her aunt had given up trying to force the man's presence on her. Relaxing, she began to read through the program for today's service. Suddenly Sarah gave her a sharp nudge.

"Look who just arrived," her aunt whispered and indicated the pew across the aisle with a shift of her eyes.

Peering over her aunt's shoulder, Irene saw Murdock Parnell seating himself in the far corner of the last pew across the aisle. He looked imposing in a suit, she thought. He was also incredibly handsome, she found herself adding.

Hearing the two women talking, Jeremy spotted Murdock and waved. The man acknowledged the boy with a friendly wink and a nod but made no move to join them.

I was right about him wanting to be left alone, Irene told herself and turned her attention to finding the first hymn scheduled to be sung.

But as the service began, she discovered herself surreptitiously glancing in Murdock Parnell's direction. She forced her attention back to the minister. But not more than a couple of minutes later, her gaze again returned to the man. This time, he noticed her looking his way and raised a questioning eyebrow as if he found her interest unexpected.

Immediately she jerked her gaze to the front of the church. A prickling on the side of her neck caused her to look back to discover he was still watching. As she quickly returned her attention to the pulpit, the prickling stopped. Feigning a concern for Jeremy's collar, she played at folding it neatly to allow herself to again covertly glance at Murdock Parnell. His full concentration was now directed at the minister.

Which is where mine should be, she scolded herself. Still, she found it impossible to focus on the sermon. She couldn't stop recalling how aware she'd been of Murdock's gaze. It had felt almost like a physical touch. Her attention threatened to wander back to him. It was as if she actually enjoyed observing him. This had got to be one of those "female things," she reasoned. Her hormones were, for some reason, overreacting. Any other good-looking male will illicit the same response, she assured herself. To prove this, she let her gaze roam over the rest of the assemblage.

Howard Chambers was a good-looking man by anyone's standards, she acknowledged searching him out. But finding him, she was forced to admit she had no interest in looking at him. He knows he's handsome and expects women to ogle him and because of that I don't really find him attractive, she rationalized.

Systematically she scanned the rest of the congregation. None of the other men, either married or single, caused her to feel any pleasure simply by their appearance. They bore me because I'm used to seeing them on a weekly basis, she reasoned. There is nothing special about Murdock Parnell, she told herself and determinedly ignored him during the remainder of the service.

But to her chagrin, the moment the service was over and she rose to leave, she had to fight to keep her gaze from turning immediately to him. Keeping her eyes cast downward, she concentrated on putting away the hymnal as she followed Jeremy out of the pew.

"Morning, Mr. Parnell," the boy suddenly said cheerfully.

Irene's gaze fell on a pair of expensive, highly polished black leather shoes. It traveled upward along the neat crease of the leg of a pair of dark gray suit pants to a finely tailored jacket, then to Murdock's face.

"Morning," he replied, his gaze taking in her, Jeremy and Sarah.

Irene noticed that while there was warmth in his eyes when his attention was on Sarah and Jeremy, they became cool when they were on her. Which suits me just fine, she affirmed, returning his greeting with an equally polite but distant one. Then giving Jeremy a push toward the door, she forced her son to continue on his way.

The day was clear and the sun bright. There was a wintery nip in the air but it wasn't uncomfortable. Normally Irene enjoyed taking a few minutes after church to visit with people out on the front lawn and today was a beautiful one for just that. But this morning she was acutely aware of Murdock exiting behind her. An uncomfortable curl of displeasure formed deep within her when two of the currently single women in the congregation scurried up to him and

introduced themselves. This was followed by an overwhelming desire to leave as quickly as possible. I simply
don't enjoy seeing women throwing themselves at a handsome man, she told herself as her annoyance with the
women grew in spite of her attempt to ignore the trio.

But Sarah refused to be rushed. She spotted Petunia Pe-
ters, whom she'd met on previous visits to Hares Burrow,
and insisted on stopping to say hello.

Keeping her back toward Murdock, Irene forced a smile
as she, too, exchanged greetings with Petunia. To her relief,
the woman had left a pot roast in the oven and needed to
hurry home to tend to it.

"Shall we head home now, also?" Irene suggested
strongly as Petunia hurried away.

Sarah was looking past her niece and the smile that had
been on her face had changed to a frown. "I think we
should make some attempt to rescue Murdock first."

Irene glanced over her shoulder to see that two more unattached females had sought him out and he was now surrounded. "He looks perfectly happy to me," she said,
noting the crooked smile on Murdock's face.

Sarah frowned at her. "That smile is definitely an 'I need
to be rescued' one," she insisted.

"Murdock Parnell is a man who can take care of himself," Irene argued.

"We'll just see." Sarah looked down at Jeremy. "You go
over and ask him if he's going to be needing to purchase
some worms this afternoon. If he says he will and he'll talk
to you later then you come right back because that'll mean
your mother is right and he doesn't want to be taken away
from his gathering harem. However, if he does want to be
rescued, he'll use the opportunity to talk business with you
to escape."

"I can't believe you're willing to use your great-nephew for such an underhanded mission," Irene fumed.

"We're only trying to help," Jeremy spoke up quickly, obviously looking forward to the role he'd been assigned to play.

"Run along," Sarah instructed, giving him a little nudge before Irene could order her son not to participate.

Refusing to watch, Irene kept her back to Murdock as Jeremy jogged across the lawn to him. She heard him asking Murdock about the purchase of the worms. Then she heard Murdock excusing himself from the group of females. A rush of pleasure swept through her. She saw Sarah giving her an "I told you so" look and grimaced sheepishly.

Sarah suddenly grinned. "Murdock, how nice to see you," she said. "I'm so sorry Jeremy pulled you away from your bevy of beauties."

Irene was startled by how honest this last remark sounded. I'll have to ask Sarah if she's done any stage acting, she thought dryly. Then Sarah was forgotten as the realization that Murdock was now joining them struck her. Mentally she groaned as she forced a smile.

"If you're going directly home, I'll just stop by on my way back," he was saying to Jeremy. "Otherwise, I'll come by later."

"We're going straight home," Jeremy replied, beaming with excitement.

Obviously he enjoyed the game, Irene noted, feeling mildly irritated with both her son and aunt. All morning she'd been trying to avoid Murdock and just when she thought she was going to escape, they'd managed to bring him into their group.

"If you don't have any plans for dinner, you might as well join us," Sarah abruptly invited. "Of course, if you prefer your own cooking, we'll understand. But my niece has made a wonderful stew and I made an apple-and-rhubarb pie fresh this morning. I'm also going to make some jalapeño corn bread to give the meal a little added zest."

"Yes, please come," Jeremy begged. "We've got ice cream if you don't like pie and Mom's stew is really good."

Irene could feel Murdock watching her. He'll say no, she assured herself, then Jeremy gave her a nudge.

"You want Mr. Parnell to come to dinner, too, don't you?" he insisted.

"Yes, of course," she heard herself saying to please her son.

Jeremy turned back to Murdock. "It'd be great to have another man at the table."

Irene saw the hesitation on Murdock's face. Then Jeremy gave him that wistful look that nearly always caused her to cave in to her son's wishes. Apparently it worked on Murdock as well. With a comradely smile, the man said, "I've never had apple-and-rhubarb pie or jalapeño corn bread. And I do like a good stew. I'd be happy to join you."

Irene was very aware that Murdock's full attention had been on her aunt and son while he accepted the invitation. Clearly her presence was of little interest to him. And his was of no interest to her, she added.

"You might as well come straight home with us," Sarah said. "We'll be eating as soon as I can get my corn bread cooked."

"Can I ride with Mr. Parnell?" Jeremy pleaded. His eyes filled with admiration, he studied the man. "Aunt Sarah found your picture in a magazine. You're a hero."

"I just did what I could," Murdock replied stiffly.

Irene was forced to admit there was no false modesty behind Murdock's words. He was the true hero type, she mused. He'd simply done what he felt had to be done and wasn't comfortable taking any credit for having done it. Jack had been like that. A hard, cold knot formed in the pit of her stomach.

The fascination in Jeremy's eyes grew. "I'll bet you weren't scared at all."

Murdock ruffled the boy's hair. "You'd lose that bet. I was scared. Real scared."

Jeremy seemed to think about this for a moment, then nodded as if approving Murdock's reaction. "I'd have been scared too. My grandpa Galvin says it's all right to be scared just so long as you don't freeze up."

"Your grandfather is a wise man," Sarah said.

Irene saw her aunt regarding her pointedly and knew Sarah was thinking that Irene had allowed the fear of facing another loss like the one she'd suffered with Jack to cause her to freeze up inside. Well, maybe she had, but there was nothing wrong with protecting herself, Irene argued silently.

"What did it feel like? The earthquake, I mean," Jeremy asked.

"Like we were all going to die," Murdock replied.

Irene caught the uneasy edge in Murdock's voice and realized he didn't want to talk about the experience. The thought occurred to her that if she allowed Jeremy to persist, the man might decide to make an excuse and recant his agreement to join them for the dinner. But the desire to come to his aid was stronger. "I'm sure Mr. Parnell would rather think about more cheerful events," she admonished her son.

Worry that he might have offended the man showed on Jeremy's face. "I'm sorry," he apologized. "Can I still ride with you? We'll talk about fishing or something like that."

"If it's all right with your mother," Murdock stipulated.

"It's all right with you, isn't it, Mom?" Jeremy pleaded.

"Yes. Sure," Irene replied, knowing her son would be crushed if she refused her permission.

As the two males walked toward the parking lot, she and Sarah followed a few paces behind.

"Jeremy certainly seems to like Murdock," Sarah noted as the sound of Jeremy's excited voice traveled back to them.

"He doesn't usually take to strangers so quickly," Irene heard herself admitting.

"Obviously he knows a good man when he sees one," Sarah returned.

Irene cast her aunt an impatient glance. "Jeremy is growing up. I suppose it's only natural for him to want male companionship."

Sarah met the impatient glance with one of her own. "He's not the only one who could benefit from a little male companionship."

Irene gave her aunt a warning glance to let her know she was treading on unsafe ground. Then in a conversational tone, she said, "The leaves are beginning to change color. In another couple of weeks the woods should be resplendent in their fall foliage."

"Resplendent," Sarah agreed, clearly getting the message that it was time to change the subject.

Following Irene Galvin's car, Murdock wondered why in the world he'd accepted a dinner invitation from Mrs. Winter Chill. Well, it hadn't really been from her, he reminded himself.

"Sounds like you had fun," he said, as Jeremy paused in the middle of telling about his trip to Alaska to visit his grandma and grandpa Orman.

Smiling, Jeremy continued with his story about cooking dinner over a campfire with his grandfather.

Good kid, Murdock thought. Obviously Mrs. Icicle was a good mother. He had, he was forced to admit, actually observed that she did have a warm side where her son and her aunt were concerned. But, her reactions to him were that of the most hard-shelled woman he'd ever crossed paths with. Normally he admired women who were independent. But not women who were so inflexible, they couldn't bend a little and Mrs. Irene Galvin reminded him of an iron rod—a very strong iron rod.

He frowned at himself. Why he was even allowing her to occupy so much of his mind was a mystery. The aunt was pleasant company and so was the boy. He would concentrate on them, enjoy the meal, then leave.

He had just finished forming this plan of action when they reached the Galvin home. But as he pulled in and parked, he found his attention drawn to the cold Mrs. Galvin. Nice legs, flashed through his mind as he watched her climb out of her car. The wind whipped her loose flowing hair around her face. Reaching up she combed the thick black tresses back with her fingers. He didn't think he'd ever seen hair glisten like that in the sunlight. She straightened and he got a full view of her profile. Very nice figure, he admitted. Again he frowned at himself. The woman was an iceberg! Besides, hadn't he just decided he would not give her a second thought?

"You want to see where I raise my worms?" Jeremy asked, reminding Murdock of his presence.

"Sure," Murdock replied, ordering himself to keep his eyes off Irene Galvin.

"Mom!"

Irene turned to her son.

"We're going to look at my worms," Jeremy called back when he saw he had her attention.

"Have fun," she returned. She'd been trying to avoid looking Murdock's way. Every time she did, she had the hardest time pulling her gaze away. Jack had been the only other man who had ever been able to hold her interest like that. "No!" she breathed under her breath.

"Having a little argument with yourself?" Sarah asked, reminding Irene of her aunt's presence. "Couldn't be because you find Murdock more attractive than you want to admit, could it?"

Irene turned to find her aunt regarding her with a gleam in her eyes. "I am not having an argument with myself," she replied firmly.

Sarah gave her an "I don't believe that for a minute" look. "I really don't understand where you got such a stubborn streak."

Irene smiled wryly. "My mother says I got it from your side of the family."

Sarah's back straightened. "We Ormans are not stubborn. We're simply determined. When we know what we want, we refuse to be deterred."

Triumph showed in Irene's eyes. "That's exactly right."

Sarah frowned. "I suppose you think you've outsmarted me, don't you?"

"I'm merely trying to make my point," Irene returned, hoping that now Sarah would respect her wishes.

Her aunt breathed a resigned sigh. "Guess I'd better get busy mixing that corn bread while you reheat your stew."

Following Sarah inside, Irene drew a relieved breath. She was sure that her aunt finally understood that any matchmaking would be unproductive and unwanted.

Sarah had gotten the message, Irene observed. During the meal her aunt had guided the conversation to Murdock but she'd gone no further than to ask him about his work and his family. As the article in the magazine had said, he confirmed that he developed computer systems and saw that they were properly installed. Where his family was concerned, he informed them that he'd been raised in Memphis, Tennessee, but now his parents lived in Florida. He had a sister in Texas and a brother in Arizona.

Early on, Irene had given up trying not to look at him. Continuing to attempt to ignore him would be impolite and much too obvious. Trying a new tactic to counter the unwanted allurement she was experiencing, she searched for annoying habits. To her chagrin he didn't seem to have any that she found particularly irritating. However, it did help that when he looked her way, a coolness entered his eyes. Obviously he wasn't the least bit attracted to her.

As the meal ended and she saw an avenue of escape, she said, "I'll clean up." Her gaze took in her aunt and Jeremy. "You two can entertain Mr. Parnell."

"We can play a game on the computer," Jeremy suggested quickly, already pushing his chair away from the table.

Sarah cast Irene a covert frown of reproval, then turning to Murdock, she smiled sweetly. "Well, I never pass up an opportunity to spend time with a handsome and charming man."

Murdock's gaze leveled on Irene. "Are you sure you don't want some help with these dishes?"

The sincerity in his voice surprised her. She was certain he was anxious to be free of her company and the continued coolness in his eyes assured her she was right in this assessment. "I'm sure," she replied.

"Come on," Jeremy urged, reaching up and taking the man's hand.

"No sense in arguing with a mule or Irene once their minds are made up," Sarah interjected.

Irene flushed. "I'm not that difficult," she said defensively.

Murdock smiled dryly. "It's been my experience that once any woman sets her mind to something, everyone else should just get out of her way." Putting action to his words, he allowed Jeremy to lead him out of the kitchen.

With a final grimace that seemed to say, "I can't believe you're letting this one get away," Sarah followed.

Alone in the kitchen, Irene began clearing the table. Through the door, she heard blips and knew they were at the computer busily involved in one of Jeremy's games. Her son's laughter told her he was enjoying himself.

She heard Murdock's answering laugh. It was a nice laugh, she found herself admitting. He's a nice man, she was forced to add. Her jaw tensed. But she wasn't looking for a man. And he sure wasn't looking her way.

Ordering herself to concentrate on the dishes, she busied herself cleaning up the kitchen. To her dismay, she was finished in record time. You can't hide out in here, she admonished herself as she stood staring at the door through which she could still hear Sarah, Jeremy and Murdock at the computer. But the thought of joining them caused her muscles to tighten. She hated admitting that Murdock unnerved her so badly, but he did.

Again a solution presented itself. With only a nod in the direction of the three game players, she continued through the living room and into her bedroom. There she changed into a pair of jeans, a shirt and her boots. Next she pulled her hair back, binding it at her nape with a rubber band. Then striding down the hall, she reentered the living room. "I've got a couple of chores I need to take care of," she said over her shoulder as she strode through that room and was in the kitchen before any of the three could even respond.

Not even pausing, she grabbed her coat off the peg by the back door and stepped outside as she pulled it on. The brisk air felt good. She was angry with herself for behaving so cowardly. I merely want to survive on my own terms and that man is having a disturbing effect on me, she told herself, defending her actions. However, in a few days, he'd be gone and she'd be able to return to her former peaceful existence. All she had to do was stay out of his way as much as possible until then.

Still, even out of the house and away from him, her muscles remained taut. The need for some manual labor to relieve her stress was strong. Murdock had been building fires in the fireplace. He probably needed more split logs and some kindling, she reasoned. And, with him being at her place, now was a good time to go over to the Brockman house and make sure he had a supply of both.

"I can't believe I'm letting him affect me this way," she muttered under her breath as she strode down the road. "He obviously doesn't even find me attractive. He's no threat."

Still she couldn't relax. Reaching the Brockman place, she went around back to the wood pile. The already split logs and kindling were nearly gone. Congratulating herself on guessing correctly, she began to work.

She'd barely begun rebuilding the stack of ready-to-burn wood when the sound of a car caught her attention. The tension that had been relieved by the physical labor returned. Silently she hoped Murdock would simply go inside and leave her alone.

"What the devil do you think you're doing?"

Irene drew a disgruntled breath as she realized her wish had not been answered. Completing the swing with the small sledgehammer, she hit the maul and split the piece of wood on the chopping block. Then turning to face Murdock, she said calmly, "I'm splitting wood for the fireplace."

He frowned down at her. "I can split my own fire-wood."

She met his frown with one of her own. "It's my job."

Impatience flickered in Murdock's eyes. "Look, I'm all for women with the pioneer spirit, but I really think you're taking this a bit too far. I really don't mind splitting my wood myself."

Irene's shoulders squared with proud defiance. "I get paid to do this, Mr. Parnell. And I believe in earning my money."

For a moment he regarded her in silence, then a flicker of amusement showed in his eyes. "I never argue with a woman holding implements of destruction." Abruptly he turned and left.

Irene knew he thought she was being unreasonable. And maybe she had been a little too harsh and bullheaded, she admitted. But learning to be independent had been a diffi-cult struggle. Besides this was her job. Trying not to think about the man, she picked up another log.

Inside, Murdock frowned as he peered at the lake. He could hear Irene Galvin chopping wood. His male ego urged him to go out there and insist on taking over the task.

In the next instant amusement again flickered in his eyes. That could be real dangerous, he warned himself. That lady knew how to use that maul and mallet. And there was an ax lying nearby.

He raked a hand through his hair. She looked kind of cute swinging that hammer, he found himself admitting. Imme-diately he shook off that thought. Toward him the woman was as cold as a winter's day and there was nothing appeal-ing about that.

Chapter Five

Irene stood on her back porch staring indecisively at the lake. It was Monday morning. Well, just barely morning. The sun was only now beginning to cast its rays over the horizon. To her left she could still see the pale silhouette of the moon in the nearly cloudless sky. This was a perfect morning for fishing.

Her gaze shifted to the Brockman place. A patch of fog had formed around their dock making it impossible for her to accurately determine if their boat was still moored there. However, she reasoned that either Murdock Parnell was already on the lake fishing or would be going out soon. To get an early start had been the reason he'd purchased the worms from her son yesterday afternoon. "And with any luck he'll stay out on the lake long enough for me to clean the Brockman house," she murmured under her breath.

"Morning." Jeremy's voice broke into her thoughts.

"Morning," she returned, smiling warmly and giving her son a hug before ushering him inside, out of the chilly morning air.

"Just in case Mr. Parnell uses up all the worms he bought yesterday before I get home from school, I'm going to set out another can for him to use this afternoon," he informed her as he seated himself at the table. "They're a gift so don't charge him."

"And I'll make a few extra biscuits," Sarah said, casting a "good morning" smile over her shoulder to Irene before returning her attention to the bowl in front of her. "He liked my jalapeño corn bread. I hope these aren't too bland for him."

Irene looked over at the cutting board to see her aunt chopping up stuffed green olives. Already chopped was a small pile of scallions. "I doubt they'll be too bland."

"I wanted to add some cheddar cheese but couldn't find any," Sarah complained.

Those biscuits should wake up a person's taste buds, Irene thought with a mental grin. "I'll take them over when I go to clean the house today," she offered, determined not to give Sarah another excuse to ask Murdock to stop by their place. A sudden mischievousness tickled through her. "Unless you've changed your mind and would like to take them over yourself later today so you can spend a little time flirting with him." Her words had come out playfully and she'd meant them that way. But the sudden thought that maybe her aunt had decided that Murdock might be Mr. Right caused a curl of displeasure very much like the one she'd experienced outside the church when the bevy of single women had surrounded Murdock. Grudgingly she was forced to admit it felt very much like jealousy. Determinedly she ignored it.

"You can take them over," Sarah replied, continuing to concentrate on her baking.

A wistfulness entered Jeremy's eyes. "He'd make a great father, don't you think?"

The wishing she heard in her son's voice shook Irene. She'd tried hard to provide him with all the love and emotional support a child could want. "I thought we were doing just fine on our own," she said stiffly.

Jeremy flushed. "We are," he assured her. "It's just that sometimes it's nice for a guy to have another man around."

Mentally she sighed. Her son was growing up. "I could ask your uncle Bill to stop by more often," she volunteered.

Jeremy shook his head. "Nah. He talks too much. He never listens."

Walter Nevins came into Irene's mind. Walter had been a friend of Jack's. He was a quiet man, a good man. He'd waited until a year after Jack's death then asked her out. She'd explained that she wasn't interested in dating anyone and they'd remained friends. "How about Walter?" she suggested.

Jeremy shook his head. "Nah. He's real nice but he's boring."

He gazed wistfully at the back door and she knew he was thinking of Murdock. Her jaw hardened. She loved Jeremy dearly but inviting Murdock Parnell into their lives was too much for him to ask. "Maybe you can spend more time with your grandfathers next summer," she said.

Hearing Sarah shoving the biscuits into the oven, Irene turned to her with a look that warned her aunt not to argue in favor of increasing Murdock's participation in their lives. Sarah smiled warmly at Jeremy. "I know your grandfathers would like to see you more."

"Yeah, I guess that would be fun," he conceded. Still, his gaze again shifted to the back door and the wistfulness returned.

"Do you want a scrambled egg or a fried egg to go with your biscuits?" Sarah asked, pulling his attention back to his breakfast.

"Fried," he replied, going to the refrigerator and taking out strawberry jam for the biscuits.

Now that should make an interesting combination, Irene thought, choosing to focus on her son's eating habits and put Murdock out of her mind. Watching her son waiting for his breakfast, what truly amazed her was that she knew Jeremy would try one of Sarah's biscuits without any encouragement. If she'd attempted a combination like that, he'd have turned up his nose and run into the other room. And men claim that women are difficult to understand, she mused.

A little later, as they finished eating, Irene glanced at the clock. "Go brush your teeth," she ordered Jeremy. "We need to leave soon so you don't miss the school bus."

Nodding, he shoved his chair away from the table, then dashed for the door.

As soon as he was gone, Sarah turned to her niece. "I know this is going to sound as if I've done a hundred-and-eighty-degree turn but I haven't. I'd still like to see you start dating again. But I don't want to see you dating a man simply for Jeremy's sake. You've provided him with a good home and plenty of love. He'll be just fine. For you to marry or even date someone because of your son's wishes would not be fair to any of you."

"Thank you," Irene said with sincerity. "I've told myself that many times, but it helps to hear someone else say it."

Sarah's expression grew stern. "However, as I have mentioned before, you should keep in mind that one day Jeremy will leave to have a life of his own. Are you sure you don't want someone to share the rest of your days with?"

"If that's what it takes to be my own woman, then yes," Irene replied with conviction.

Sarah rose and gave her a hug. "Well, if I don't find my Mr. Right, we can grow old together."

Returning her aunt's hug, Irene wasn't certain whether to consider this a consoling thought or a threat.

"How about if I drive Jeremy to school this morning?" Sarah suggested as she released her niece and began clearing the table. "I need to stop by the post office and there's a little shopping I want to do."

"I know he'd like that," Irene replied, thinking that the tide seemed to have truly turned in her favor. Not having to walk Jeremy to the bus stop and wait until his bus arrived would save her half an hour at least, probably more. "And that will allow me to get an early start on the Brockman house," she added gratefully.

Sarah cast her a sideways glance. "Think you can get done before Murdock gets back from fishing?"

That her aunt had seen through her ploy didn't surprise Irene. No sense in lying to Sarah, she decided. "I hope so."

A short while later she was knocking on the front door of the Brockman house. To her relief there was no answer. Obviously she'd guessed right about Murdock going fishing. Leaving the worms on the front porch, she entered.

Doing laundry was not a regular part of her job. She did however do the kitchen, bathroom and bed linens when necessary. When the Brockmans were here for extended lengths of time, they usually did their own. It was only after they'd left that she'd come over and do up any they'd left unlaundered. However, not knowing Murdock's habits, she decided she should check the upstairs hamper. If she started a load of bath and kitchen linens now, she could have them washed and dried by the time she was ready to leave.

But as she reached the upstairs landing, she heard a groan as if someone was in pain. There was no doubt in her mind that that someone was Murdock. Next he issued a gruff growl. Then came a harsh, startled sounding "No!" followed by a command to duck.

Dread mingled with pain in those words. Terrified something horrible was happening, she grabbed one of the antique swords Horace had hanging on the hall wall for decoration and raced toward the bedroom from which the voice was emanating. Reaching the open door, she came to an abrupt halt. Murdock was alone inside lying on his bed. From the waist down he was wrapped in a sheet. From the waist up, he was bare. He was tossing and turning, fighting a battle in his sleep. A grim look was etched deeply into his features.

"No," he growled again and the despair in his voice shook her.

He twisted on his side and thrust his arm upward as if to ward off something from above. The arm he was using to protect himself from the invisible danger was the one with the bandage. It banged against the headboard and pain flashed across his face.

An answering pain seemed to pierce her. Quickly setting the sword aside, she crossed the room to the bed. "Murdock. Mr. Parnell," she said tersely, taking hold of his shoulder and forcing him onto his back hoping to prevent him from hurting himself again. "Wake up. You're dreaming."

He opened his eyes and stared up at her. For a long moment, there was only puzzlement in those brown depths as if he hadn't quite separated reality from his nightmare. Then he drew a shaky breath and his body sank into the bed, all the fight gone out of him. "Mrs. Galvin?"

"I came to clean. I thought you would be out fishing on the lake," she said in answer to the question in his voice. She noticed his hair was wet with sweat and there were beads of perspiration on his forehead. Releasing her hold on his shoulders, she combed the wet locks back from his face and wiped his brow with her hand. To her relief he didn't seem to be running a temperature. "Are you all right?" she asked.

"It was just a nightmare," he said gruffly. "I've been having them ever since the quake. That's why I came here instead of going home. Didn't want to upset my mother." He drew a calming breath. "Luckily they're getting farther and farther apart."

Irene was still standing over him, one hand on his shoulder and the other on his brow. As the realization that he really was all right sank in, she became acutely aware of the enticing texture of his skin and the hard musculature of his shoulder. A fire began to kindle within her. Abruptly she straightened and took a step back. A flush of embarrassment spread from her neck upward. Unexpectedly she found herself wondering if he was wearing anything under that sheet. The conclusion that most likely he wasn't or, if he was, it was very little, caused the fire to blaze hotter. "I'll come back later to clean," she said, backing toward the door.

He eased himself into a sitting position on the bed. "No. As long as you're here, you might as well get it done. I'm sure not going back to sleep. One nightmare a night is enough for me."

I'm lusting after the man, she wailed, wanting to run. But pride refused to allow her to retreat in such an undignified manner. "I'll just collect the used towels from the bathroom and put out fresh ones. Then I'll start cleaning downstairs," she said stiffly. That's dignified enough, she told herself and quickly turned and left.

He was neat, she noted, as she grabbed up the used towels, then hung fresh ones. He was also a hunk, she admitted, the image of his naked upper body seeming to be permanently implanted in her mind. Mentally she ran her hand over the dark curly hairs that formed a V on his chest. Forcefully she shook herself. Never had she had such wanton thoughts since Jack died.

Get this house cleaned and get out of here, she ordered herself. Putting action to this command, she quickly made her way downstairs.

Murdock lay in bed listening to Irene Galvin's footsteps. The compassion he'd seen in her eyes when he'd woken burned in his mind. He'd known she was capable of warm feelings. He'd seen her show them toward her son and her aunt. But he'd never expected to see that warmth turned on him.

Then there was her touch. The way she'd combed back his hair and felt his brow had been incredibly soothing. Usually the horror of these nightmares stayed with him for hours after he'd woken. Admittedly he still felt shaken but he didn't need to rush into the bathroom to throw up.

And her compassion and her warmth were not all he'd noticed. He was certain that deep in the blue depths of her eyes, he'd seen the spark of desire. And it was the memory of that fire that continued to ward off the lingering images of death and destruction as he climbed out of bed.

Downstairs in the Brockmans' kitchen, Irene stood staring at the coffeepot. While she'd been loading the washing machine, the thought that she should start some coffee brewing for Murdock had nagged at her. He certainly looked as if he needed it. Feelings of protectiveness welled within her. You're treading on dangerous ground, she warned herself. Just do your work and get out of here.

Still, she continued to stare at the coffeepot. "I'm not going to have any peace until I get it brewing," she muttered under her breath and strode to the counter.

She was just plugging in the percolator when Murdock entered. He was wearing jeans and a sweatshirt. His feet were bare, his hair uncombed and his face unshaven. "Thanks," he said when he noticed what she was up to. "I like to get the coffee started before I shave."

She noted the dark circles under his eyes. She also noticed that his usual authoritarian bearing was missing. That, coupled with his unkempt state made him look like a man who needed a friend. She didn't really want to be that friend, still, she heard herself asking, "Are you really all right?"

A self-conscious, crooked grin tilted one corner of his mouth. "Yeah."

Having given her this assurance, she expected him to leave and go shave. In truth, she fervently hoped that he would. He was much too appealing with that vulnerable expression on his face.

Instead he leaned against the doorjamb and raked a hand through his hair. "Thanks for waking me."

Studying him, she knew he needed to talk and she'd never been able to turn away from anyone in pain. "I guess the earthquake must have been a pretty devastating experience," she said, sympathetically.

The lopsided grin returned. "You could say that." He shoved his hands into the pockets of his jeans and leaned his head back against the door frame. A distant look came over his features. "I can't seem to forget the faces of the dead. It happened so suddenly. We had no real warning. There was a cluster of us around one of the computer terminals in a back office. I was teaching the others how to use the system. There were three men and a woman. Suddenly the building shifted. Then it seemed to move beneath our feet as if someone had picked it up and was shaking it. The walls started cracking and pieces began to fall. Then the roof was caving in on us. I heard women and children screaming and crying in panic. I remembered there had been several customers in the outer room.''

Irene felt his anguish as intensely as if it was her own. She tried to think of something to say. Everything she thought of sounded like a cliché. ''What happened then?'' she heard herself asking.

''I was sitting in a chair. It slid out from under me and I ended up under the table the computer was sitting on. One of the other men, Carlos, had the presence of mind to duck under a nearby desk.'' He swallowed hard. ''The quake lasted only seconds but it seemed like forever. When it did stop, we discovered that the others in the room hadn't been so lucky. The two men had been killed by falling debris.'' His complexion turned ashen. ''A filing cabinet had fallen on the woman but she was still alive. Carlos and I tried to free her, but suddenly she just shuddered and . . . she was gone.''

He paused and rubbed his face hard, then shoved his hands back into the pockets of his jeans. Watching him, Irene knew his mind was now fully back in that bank. A haunted look came into his eyes as he continued to relive the trauma.

''Carlos said we had to get out of there. We'd done what we could and there could be an aftershock that would bring down the rest of the building. We made our way to the main room. People were digging themselves out from the rubble.

There was a woman with her leg pinned beneath a long marble-topped counter that had come loose from the wall and fallen. I yelled for Carlos to help me but he was already helping an elderly woman get her husband outside. I went over and somehow managed to lift the marble slab enough for the woman to squirm out from under it. Her leg was badly injured. She couldn't walk. I grabbed her up. I could feel her holding back a scream of pain. I started toward the entrance. There was a young child sitting beside the body of a woman. It was a little girl and she was sobbing. I picked her up, too. She kept screaming for her mother and kicking at me trying to free herself but I knew I had to get her out of there. Then we were outside.''

He paused to draw a harsh breath. ''There were people sitting in the street sobbing. And there were bodies. The little girl kept screaming for her mother and when I put her down, she tried to run back inside. A woman standing a few feet away suddenly began yelling a name and ran and grabbed the child and hugged her. Turned out the woman was her aunt. The child continued to scream and try to break free. I promised her I'd go back in and get her mother—that seemed to calm her.''

A shadow of triumph eased the grimness of his expression. ''I was sure the woman was dead but I couldn't stand there not knowing for certain. Besides, the little girl was still trying to break free and run back inside. But when I went back in, I discovered the mother was only unconscious. I could feel her breathing. It wasn't strong breathing but it was breathing.'' The grimness returned. ''The building began to shake again. I lifted the woman and began carrying her outside. I had to step over a body. It was a man. I knew he was dead. I'd checked him on my way in. But I still remember that body more than the woman I managed to get out.''

"You did what you could. You did more than some people would," Irene said softly.

Again the self-conscious grin appeared. "Horace insisted I talk to a shrink to help get over the nightmares. That's the new company policy...everyone involved in a traumatic event has to go talk to a doctor. Anyway, the shrink told me I was suffering from guilt because I survived and others didn't."

Irene frowned. "There is no reason for you to feel guilty."

He nodded. "I know. That's what he told me, too. But it's going to take time to get the images of the dead out of my head."

Without even thinking, she approached him and rested her hand on his jaw. "You heroes all have the same problem...you want to have complete control of your world and everything in it." A rueful look came over her face. "Well, you can't take responsibility for everyone else."

"You've got me wrong, lady," he said tiredly. "All I want is a little peace of mind."

He might be looking for peace of mind but he was destroying hers, she thought as the desire to slip into his arms and reassure him with a hug grew strong. "Then I hope you find it." Just then actually realizing she was touching him, she lowered her hand and took a step back to put distance between them.

Unexpectedly he cupped her chin in his hand. "And what do you want, Mrs. Irene Galvin?" he asked gruffly.

For you to kiss me, was the answer that flashed through her mind. Her body stiffened. No! her inner voice screamed at her. This weakness she was feeling would only lead to trouble. "I need to get back to my work," she said and jerking free, she brushed past him and strode down the hall.

Watching her, Murdock felt a rush of frustration. He knew now that Irene Galvin could be a compassionate woman. He also suspected she could be a very passionate one as well. Just before she'd fled, he'd again seen the flames of desire begin to glow in her eyes.

But he'd also seen the way her jaw had hardened into a determined line. That coupled with her quick withdrawal made it evident she was not willing to give in to her more passionate nature. I suppose she thinks she would be betraying her dead husband, he decided. An unexpected jab of jealousy for the late Mr. Galvin startled him. He frowned. If she preferred to live with the memory of a ghost then he wished her well, he assured himself and went upstairs to shave.

Irene was dusting the living room when she heard him descending the stairs. She'd been trying to push the image of his tired grim face from her mind. She'd also been trying not to think of how enticing the rough texture of his whiskers had felt beneath her palm. Ignore him and get on with your work, she ordered herself as he came down the hall. But instead, she looked up as he passed. Seeing her looking his way, he paused and raised a questioning eyebrow.

"Sarah sent some biscuits and Jeremy sent some worms," she informed him. "He said to tell you the worms were a gift."

A mischievous smile suddenly appeared on his face. "I think I'll have the biscuits for breakfast. The worms I'll save for the fish," he replied.

She found herself grinning back. "Funny, real funny," she returned dryly. The thought that he might also want to feed the biscuits to the fish crossed her mind. "The biscuits have olives and onions in them," she warned.

A dubious expression replaced his smile. "Interesting combination."

"Would you like me to scramble you some eggs to go with them?" Irene paled. She couldn't believe she'd said that.

Panic swept through her. She refused to give in to the attraction she was feeling for this man. Before he could respond, she glanced at her watch. "Oh, sorry. I'm running late." Turning her back to him, she stuck her dust cloth in her belt and quickly switched on the vacuum.

Murdock frowned thoughtfully as he continued into the kitchen. Just before she'd turned away, he'd seen panic in her eyes. He was sure of that. He frightened her. But why? The thought that he might actually be causing those thick walls of ice she kept around herself to melt brought a sense of pleasure. He pictured her in his arms, her thick black hair cascading over her shoulders. Desire sparked to life within him.

"You're here to rest and find peace of mind," he cautioned himself, as he opened the refrigerator and took out a carton of eggs. "You don't need to tangle with a woman who still carries a torch for her dead husband."

The problem was, he admitted, he was much too aware of Mrs. Irene Galvin. Even out of his view, he could picture her clearly. "Forget her," he ordered himself as he broke an egg into the skillet.

Irene quickly finished cleaning the downstairs and went upstairs. She'd hoped putting more distance between herself and Murdock would make her less aware of his presence. She was wrong. A faint scent of his after-shave lingered in the guest bathroom. Somewhere deep inside embers of desire began to kindle once again.

"I'm doing just fine on my own and that's the way I like it," she affirmed under her breath.

But as she entered the bedroom he was using, the embers grew hotter. He'd made the bed, but in her mind's eye she saw him there, wrapped only in a sheet. The remembered texture of his skin and the strength of his shoulders ignited fingers of flame. "No," she seethed under her breath, and quickly vacuumed and dusted.

Willing herself to concentrate only on her chores, she finished in record time. Noting that Murdock was sitting on the back porch, she hoped to get out of the house without encountering him again. But as she finished putting away the laundry he sought her out.

"Thank Sarah for the biscuits," he said, a gleam of amusement in his eyes. "They added spice to my breakfast." The amusement faded into a warm smile. "And thank Jeremy for the worms."

The soft look on his face caused Irene's heart to skip a beat. Frantically she fought to keep her defensive shield in place. "I will," she said stiffly. "Now if you'll excuse me, I've got work at home to take care of."

As she walked briskly away from the house, she felt a prickling on the back of her neck. She did not need to look back to know the sensation was being caused by Murdock watching her. Again her awareness of the man shook her. Concentrate on Jeremy and Sarah, she ordered herself.

Murdock studied her thoughtfully as she strode down the road. Again he'd seen the panic in her eyes. And again a sense of masculine pleasure spread through him. The memory of waking to her touch sparked a fire and he found himself wondering how her lips would taste. "She's trouble with a capital *T*," he growled at himself. "I came here to fish and rest." Jerking his gaze away from the swing of her hips, he headed around to the back porch to get his equipment.

Irene drew a tired breath. For the remainder of this day, after leaving the Brockman house, she'd been reasonably successful in her attempt to put Murdock Parnell out of her mind. But once Jeremy was in bed and she and Sarah were watching television, a restlessness had filled her. The pain she'd seen on Murdock's face had come back to haunt her. Going into the kitchen for a cup of coffee, she'd gotten as far as picking up the pot. Then abruptly she'd set it down, grabbed her coat and stepped out on the back porch.

Now, staring across the lake, she wondered if he was getting a better night's sleep tonight. A picture of her there with him, keeping his mind off those nightmarish images filled her mind. A heat swept through her.

"Nice night." Sarah's voice broke into her thoughts.

The image shattered. "A gorgeous night," she returned with forced enthusiasm.

Sarah studied her narrowly. "Are you ready to tell me what's bothering you?"

Irene managed an innocent look. "Nothing is bothering me."

Sarah regarded her impatiently. "Ever since you came back from cleaning the Brockman house this morning, you've been perky."

Irene couldn't stop herself from smiling. "Perky?"

"Perky," Sarah repeated. "For as long as I can remember, whenever something is gnawing at you, you've tried to cover it up by getting perky."

"Maybe I have been a little bit overly enthusiastic and cheerful," Irene conceded. "But I'm just so happy to have you here, I want you to know it."

"Young lady," Sarah said sternly. "While I'm flattered, I'm not fooled. Normally when you're pleased about something, you're calm, easygoing with a ready smile. Today, you've been too sharply cheerful . . . you've been *Perky*."

Irene breathed a resigned sigh. Sarah knew her too well. "When I went over to the Brockmans' place today, Murdock was still asleep. He was having a nightmare about the earthquake."

Sarah nodded, her expression becoming that of a professional nurse. "That's normal. He's been through a trauma. Dreams are one way of working through the residual fear and panic."

Concern etched itself deeply into Irene's features. "He was thrashing around. I had to wake him before he hurt himself. Later, he told me about the quake and the horror he'd seen. I wanted to help, to say something that would lessen his anguish. But I couldn't think of anything. I felt useless."

"Careful," Sarah cautioned with a soft smile. "In a minute you'll be admitting you care for him."

Irene frowned. "I care *about* him. That's not the same as caring *for* him. He's been through a horrifying experience, it's only natural I should feel some compassion."

"You've been too perky for mere compassion." A coaxing quality entered Sarah's voice. "Come on, admit it. Prove to me you're not totally dead inside. You felt a spark, didn't you?"

Irene's gaze returned to the house across the lake. Again the image of Murdock in his bed, filled her mind. "It's been a long time since I've been in a bedroom with a man. And Murdock is certainly virile. It's only natural I would feel something."

Triumph glistened in Sarah's eyes. "I'm glad to know you haven't managed to totally smother your passionate side."

Irene's jaw firmed. "I admitted to feeling a spark. But I'm not going to let it turn into a blazing fire."

Sarah rewarded this declaration with a motherly smile. "Sometimes you don't have a choice."

Determination glittered in Irene's eyes. "I have a choice."

"If I were you, I'd do some hard thinking before I made any decisions," Sarah advised. "Men like Murdock Parnell don't come along every day."

A thought brought a dry smile to Irene's face. "This entire conversation is purely academic. What makes you think Murdock Parnell would even give me a second glance?"

Sarah placed an arm around her niece's shoulders. "Why wouldn't he? You're sweet, warm, intelligent with a good sense of humor, an excellent mother and homemaker, and a caring person. Granted, you can be a little stubborn at times, but no one is perfect."

"And I'm happy with my life just the way it is," Irene stated firmly. But instead of the sense of security and well-being these words generally gave her, she felt like a broken record repeating something she was getting tired of hearing. This traitorous reaction brought a rush of fear. My life might be lacking some excitement but it's safe, she reminded herself. A chilly breeze swirled around her and, in spite of the heavy jacket she was wearing, she shivered. "I think it's time we went inside," she said, heading for the door.

For a moment, Sarah hesitated as if she had more to say. Then abruptly, she smiled her best motherly smile and nodded in agreement.

A little later in her room, Irene again found herself standing at her window looking toward the Brockman house. She saw Murdock walk out onto the balcony off his bedroom. He stood there for a long while looking out at the lake and she wondered if he'd had another nightmare. She suddenly wished she was there beside him. Groaning in frustration at the strength her traitorous thoughts were gathering, she left the window and climbed into bed. But retreating into the snug haven didn't help. For the first time in a long time, as she curled up under the heavy down comforter, a feeling of loneliness threatened to overwhelm her.

Chapter Six

Late the next afternoon, Murdock was sitting in one of the several rocking chairs on the porch of the Brockman house. He was leaning back in the chair, his long legs stretched out in front of him with his feet crossed at the ankles and propped up on the wooden railing bordering the porch. In front of him was the lake with the sun glistening on its surface. A picture postcard view, he'd thought when he'd first sat down. But it wasn't the tranquil setting surrounding him that was now occupying his mind. Instead a black-haired, blue-eyed woman filled his thoughts.

The frown on his face deepened. Last night, Irene Galvin had been in his dreams. Admittedly he'd slept better than he had in weeks. And he hadn't woken in a cold sweat. Instead he'd woken with the memory of her looking at him with a heat in her eyes that had him wishing she'd truly been there with him. The woman isn't available, he told himself for the umpteenth time today.

"Hi." A cheerful young voice cut into Murdock's thoughts.

He turned to see Jeremy Galvin at the foot of the steps. "Do you mind if I join you?" the boy asked politely.

"I'd enjoy the company," Murdock replied. Anything to get Irene Galvin off his mind would be a relief, he added silently, then was forced to admit he did honestly enjoy the boy's company. Sitting on the pier the other day talking with Jeremy had reminded Murdock of the best times spent with his father . . . the quiet times when they'd sat and talked, sometimes about important things like Murdock's future and what he wanted in life and sometimes about nothing important at all.

"Nice day," Jeremy said as he pulled one of the rocking chairs closer to the rail so he could sit and prop his feet up the same as Murdock.

"How was school today? Learn anything?" Murdock asked, a grin playing at the corner of his mouth as he recalled his father asking him that same question hundreds of times.

"We talked about that pyramid thing with the seven food groups," Jeremy replied, gazing out at the lake in a good imitation of Murdock's relaxed pose. Abruptly he grinned and turned to look at Murdock. "If Aunt Sarah had added bits of bacon or sausage to her biscuits yesterday, I bet they would have fit into every group."

Murdock returned the boy's grin. "Actually, adding bacon sort of sounds good."

"Yeah," Jeremy agreed, a twinkle in his eyes. Then his expression became serious. "What do you think of my mom?"

Murdock hid his surprise at this unexpected change of subject. "She appears to be a good mother," he replied noncommittally.

Jeremy nodded. "She is." His expression grew even more serious. "But that's not what I meant." He paused for a long moment and Murdock had the distinct impression the boy was searching for a new avenue of approach. Then Jeremy asked, "Do you know about sparks? The kind between men and women?"

Murdock recalled the fire he'd seen in Irene Galvin's eyes. He also recalled the ice and wondered where this conversation was headed. "Are you talking about the fighting kind or the kind that occur when two people are attracted to each other?"

"The kind when they're attracted," Jeremy replied.

"I know a little," Murdock admitted.

Jeremy regarded him matter-of-factly. "When you first came, Mom told aunt Sarah she didn't feel any sparks. But last night I heard her say she did." He suddenly looked self-conscious. "I was supposed to be asleep but yesterday in school Bobby Harris said he saw a shooting star the night before and I thought I'd see if I could see one. I was looking out my window when I heard voices on the porch. I couldn't tell who was there so I opened my window just a little to make sure it wasn't a burglar. But I closed the window as soon as I was sure it was just Mom and Aunt Sarah."

Murdock found himself feeling pleased that Irene Galvin had actually admitted to feeling an attraction toward him. Then he recalled the way she constantly withdrew behind that protective shield she kept around herself. The woman was nothing but trouble, he again warned himself.

"Anyway," Jeremy continued, a hopefulness in his eyes. "I was wondering if maybe you felt a spark toward my mom. She's really very nice and I'd kind of like to have a dad and you and I get along real good."

Murdock wondered what Irene would say if she knew her son was out matchmaking. He guessed she would not be pleased. The sincerity in the boy's voice kept him from smiling dryly as he pictured her reaction. "It sounds as if you've given this a lot of thought. But I don't think your mother is looking for a husband."

A plea entered Jeremy's eyes. "If you did feel a spark, you could try to change her mind."

Murdock was not a man who normally backed down from a challenge, but in this case his common sense told him that would be the best path to take. "Your mother seems like a woman who knows her own mind," he replied.

"She's really terrific," Jeremy insisted.

Murdock recalled how soothing her touch had been. "I'm sure she is," he conceded. Then again he remembered how she'd drawn away from him. "But, like I said, I don't think she's in the market for a husband."

Turning his attention to the lake, Jeremy frowned resignedly. "I guess you're right." Dropping his feet from the rail, he rose. "I better get home and do my homework."

He looked so disappointed, Murdock felt like a heel. I'm just being realistic, he reasoned. He wasn't opposed to marriage. And he did feel a certain attraction toward Irene Galvin. Under other circumstances he might even have considered getting to know her better to see if they might have a future together. But he wasn't interested in a relationship haunted by the ghost of an ex-spouse.

"Bye." Jeremy waved over his shoulder without even turning to look back as he descended the stairs.

Murdock felt like a bigger heel with each passing step the boy was taking. "I'll walk you home," he said, dropping his feet and pushing himself out of the chair.

Jeremy paused to wait for him. But he didn't smile. "You don't have to. I know the way."

Murdock mussed the boy's hair. "I'd like for us to stay friends," he said and was shocked by how much this meant to him.

A crooked smile made its way across Jeremy's face. "Yeah, we're still friends," he conceded.

"Tell me more about your day at school," Murdock requested as they began to stroll slowly down the road.

"We saw a movie about spiders. It showed all different kinds and how they build their homes," Jeremy replied. He grinned playfully. "Some of the girls thought it was icky."

As they walked and Jeremy described some of the more exotic arachnids, Murdock found himself thinking he'd enjoy being a father to the boy. Then Irene Galvin's image entered his mind. The woman did have kissable looking lips. And very nice curves in all the right places he added, noticing her coming their way up the road.

"I hope Jeremy hasn't been making a nuisance of himself," she said, as the three met.

"No, he hasn't," Murdock assured her. He studied the guarded expression on her face. The iciness he'd become accustomed to seeing in her eyes was missing.

She shifted her gaze to her son. "I thought I should remind him he has homework."

"I remembered," Jeremy said. "I was on my way home to do it."

Irene motioned in the direction of their house. "Then we'd better be going." Jeremy turned to Murdock. "Do you want to walk with us?" Murdock saw the hopeful gleam in the boy's eyes.

"I'm sure Mr. Parnell has better things to do with his time," Irene interjected quickly.

Murdock heard the dismissal in her voice. She might feel a spark but she sure wasn't willing to let it become a flame, he noted. "Yeah, I should be getting back," he said.

Reaching down, he again ruffled the boy's hair. "See you tomorrow, pal."

"See you tomorrow," Jeremy returned with a look of resignation.

Turning back toward the Brockman house, Murdock discovered himself actually considering pursuing Irene Galvin. I'd be smart to leave her to her ghost, he told himself. Still, he glanced over his shoulder for a final glimpse of her.

Ignoring the momentary prickling on the back of her neck, Irene studied her son worriedly out of the corner of her eye as they walked toward their house. He was much too subdued. "Are you angry with me for not encouraging Mr. Parnell to walk with us?" she asked, breaking the silence between them.

"No, that's okay," he replied, and slipped his hand into hers as if to say he understood.

Irene knew he was telling the truth. Still, she couldn't stop feeling as if something was distressing him. "Do you have anything you want to talk about?" she asked encouragingly. "Is there something worrying you?"

"Nope," he answered quickly.

Irene knew her son well enough to know he wasn't being totally honest with her. "What were you and Mr. Parnell talking about?" she asked, keeping her voice conversational so she did not sound as if she was prying.

"Just guy stuff." He gave an exaggerated shrug. "Spiders."

Spiders were definitely "guy stuff" Irene conceded. But that exaggerated shrug made her suspicious that arachnids were not all that her son had sought Murdock Parnell out to talk about. Motherly concern nagged her.

And during the next few hours, her concern grew. Jeremy was much too quiet and periodically she saw him simply sitting, staring off into space with a wistful expression on his face.

As she and Sarah cleared the dinner dishes, she knew she was going to have to go talk to Murdock Parnell. She didn't like the idea of seeking the man out. Seeing him and Jeremy walking together down the road today, she'd felt a strong tug at her heartstrings. Murdock was definitely a threat to the lock she kept on her emotions. However, she was certain something was bothering Jeremy and she was equally certain he'd discussed whatever it was with Mr. Parnell.

"I'm going for a walk," she informed Sarah as they finished straightening the kitchen. "I have some thinking I need to do," she added, wanting to assure her solitude without revealing her destination.

"You run along," Sarah said. "Jeremy and I are going to play a game on the computer."

Satisfied they would be occupied for plenty of time, Irene grabbed her coat from the peg and left.

Halfway to the Brockman house the urge to run back home became almost overpowering. Grudgingly she admitted Murdock Parnell frightened the woman within her. She did not want that part of her awakened and he was proving to be a very strong alarm clock. However, the mother in her had to know what was bothering her son. Her jaw set in a firm line, she forced her legs to carry her onward.

Murdock sat staring at the flames consuming the logs in the fireplace. Several times this evening he'd ordered himself to put Irene Galvin out of his mind, still she lingered there. Giving up the struggle, he admitted that the woman he'd glimpsed beneath her cool exterior interested him greatly. He would like to have the opportunity to get to know that woman better.

And Jeremy's disclosure was encouraging him to pursue this interest. A self-mocking expression crossed his face. Who was he trying to kid? Even without the boy's revelation, he would have tried to break through that barrier she kept around herself. Not since his very first adolescent crush had a woman held his attention this strongly.

Irene took a deep breath and knocked on the door of the Brockman house.

Surprise registered on Murdock's face when he answered the summons. Then his expression became shuttered. "I didn't expect to find you knocking on my door," he said, stepping aside to allow her to enter.

She looked at him, expecting to see impatience for having interrupted his evening. Instead she saw only polite curiosity. "I need to know what's disturbing my son," she said bluntly, wanting only to finish her business and leave.

"Can I take your coat?"

He was smiling at her. It was a nice smile...pleasant, friendly. It encouraged her to let down her guard. She shifted uneasily. "No, I won't be here long. I simply want to know what Jeremy came here to talk to you about. My son gets a particular look on his face when he has something on his mind and he's had that look on his face all evening."

"I've got a fire going in the fireplace. Won't you, at least, sit down for a moment?" Murdock suggested.

He was studying her and his scrutiny was making her more and more nervous. The need to escape grew stronger. Maybe she was mistaken, she told herself. Maybe Jeremy didn't really have anything that was bothering him and even if he did, she should be able to convince him to tell her. "I shouldn't have come here," she said stiffly. "This is between my son and me."

"He seems to have included me in it."

She'd turned and started toward the door. Now she stopped and turned back. So she had been right. Jeremy had come to talk to Murdock Parnell about whatever was bothering him. "What is on his mind?" she asked.

Murdock moved toward her.

Irene took a couple of steps back. To her embarrassment, she backed into the wall.

Murdock frowned. "You don't need to be afraid of me."

"I'm not," she replied, honestly. It was herself and the reactions she was having to this man that frightened her. Right now, she found herself thinking that he looked incredibly kissable. Concentrate on Jeremy, she ordered herself, forcing her cool shield back into place.

Murdock took another step closer leaving less than a foot between them. "Your son has decided he wants a father and he seems to think I would be a good choice."

So do I, flashed through Irene's mind. No! her inner voice screamed back. "I'm really sorry he's been nagging you," she managed, then marveled that the sentence had come out coherently. There was a heat in his eyes that could melt a snowcap, she thought, feeling her shield turning to slush.

She started to edge her way toward the door. Murdock placed a hand against the wall blocking her retreat with his arm. "I'm flattered he thinks so highly of me. He's a terrific kid."

"He is a terrific kid," Irene agreed. When he'd placed his hand on the wall, Murdock had leaned closer to her. His warm breath teased her skin. She shoved her hands into the pockets of her coat to keep herself from acting on the impulse to trace the line of his jaw with her fingertips.

He leaned even closer. "I've been thinking that a man would be proud to have Jeremy for a son." His gaze bore into her. "You have the most gorgeous blue eyes."

Irene tried to usher her defenses. Frantically she attempted to will her wall of ice back into existence. Instead she felt herself being drawn into the warm brown depths of his eyes. "I really should be going," she murmured, but her legs refused to move.

"And you have the most kissable-looking lips I've ever seen," he persisted.

She found herself coming close to admitting she'd been thinking the same thing about him. But before she could utter anything, his mouth had found hers. The contact was light, undemanding, still fire raged through her.

Her breath locked in her lungs as she waited expectantly for the kiss to become more assertive. Instead he lifted his head away. With his free hand, he toyed with her hair, gently combing it back behind her ear. ·

His feather-light touch played havoc on her sensitized skin. The slightest brush of his fingertips sent a current of heat along her neck. Looking up into his eyes she saw a reflection of the desire he'd awakened in her. "Take off your coat. Stay awhile," he requested gruffly.

How much she wanted to do just that panicked Irene. Her hands formed fists around the fabric of her coat and she pulled the garment more securely around her. "I really can't," she said.

Impatience flickered across his features. "I'm only asking you to stay and talk. I won't press you for anything further."

"Talking with you could be dangerous." She flushed when she realized what she'd said. Somehow she found the agility to slip under his arm. Free, she again headed to the door. But as she reached for the knob, a hand as strong as a vise closed around her arm. Looking up, she saw Murdock scowling down at her, impatience mingled with frustration.

"You're too young and too vital to let yourself continue to live with a ghost," he growled.

Her back stiffened defensively. "I'm not living with a ghost."

"I know fear when I see it and I know passion. You're terrified by the emotions I've aroused in you. If you're not feeling guilty because you think you're betraying your dead husband, then why run?" he challenged.

"Because I don't ever want to feel dependent on another person again," she returned, attempting to jerk free. "It took me a long time to learn to stand on my own two feet. Jack was like you, the hero type. He took care of everything. He said he never wanted me to worry about anything. He made all the decisions in our marriage. He paid the bills, he balanced the checkbook, he even helped me pick out my clothes. When he died I was totally unprepared to take care of myself much less myself and a child. Learning to be independent was difficult. I won't give it up."

Releasing her, Murdock frowned in confusion. "I admire your independence," he said honestly. "I would never want to take that away from you."

"It's not you I'm worried about," she admitted. An anxiousness shadowed her features. "It's me."

The confusion on his face increased. "You?"

"I'm afraid I'll revert to the way I was. I'll become a dependent blob of nothing."

Murdock grinned. "I find that real hard to picture."

"Or, maybe I'd feel suffocated making even the smallest of compromises," she continued. "No relationship, especially a marriage, can work without compromises."

"You can't let the fear of the unknown rule your life," he argued.

Her back stiffened defiantly. "I like my life just the way it is." Before he could offer any further argument, she fled.

Outside, a cold wind fought her as she briskly walked away from the Brockman house. She'd lied and she knew it. She wasn't completely happy with her life the way it was. But she did feel safe.

Murdock considered going after her. The taste of her lips lingered on his. He wanted her in his arms. But he didn't want her there against her will. He wasn't ready to give up his pursuit but he knew he was going to have to go slowly. Give her space, he ordered himself.

A gust of wind so strong it rattled the windows whipped across the porch. He scowled out at the night. Opening the door, he realized the temperature had dropped drastically. He'd heard the weatherman talking about a nor'easter coming through. Grabbing his coat and car keys, he left the house.

Irene heard the car coming down the road behind her but she kept her attention focused ahead of her and continued walking.

Pulling alongside of her, Murdock rolled down his window. "Get in," he ordered.

"I enjoy walking," she returned.

"You're being unreasonably stubborn," he growled. "Get in before you freeze."

"I'm used to the cold," she growled back, continuing on her way. She knew she was being unreasonable but she didn't want to get into that car with him. Her resistance to him was too weak.

"You can get in on your own or I will physically put you in," he threatened.

This time she stopped and turned to look at him. The determination she saw on his face convinced her he was telling the truth. And the last thing she wanted was for him to touch her. Just the thought caused the fires she was trying to smother to relight. "I knew you wouldn't respect my need to be independent," she muttered, frantically hunting for reasons to bolster the barrier she was struggling to keep between them.

The frown on his face deepened. "I respect your independence. I just don't want you catching pneumonia."

Rewarding him with a haughty expression, she climbed in.

In silence he drove her home. As he pulled into her driveway, she managed a stiff, "Thank you." Then she quickly climbed out of his car and went inside.

"You're welcome," he muttered to her departing back. "She's impossible, absolutely impossible," he grumbled as he drove back to the Brockman house. "I've never expected to understand women but she's beyond anyone's comprehension. No matter what I did she would have found fault with me. If I hadn't tried to take her home, then I would have been heartless and inconsiderate. But when I did, I was infringing on her independence. The only smart thing to do is to forget her!" he concluded as he parked and stalked into the house.

"Wasn't that Murdock's car?" Sarah said as Irene entered the house through the front door.

"Yes," she answered with schooled indifference, continuing through the living room toward the kitchen.

Jeremy was playing at his computer. Immediately he jerked his attention to his mother. "You were with Mr. Parnell?"

She saw the hopefulness in his eyes. "He came along while I was walking. The weather had turned much colder and he offered me a ride home," she replied, shading the truth so as not to encourage him.

"He's real nice, don't you think?" Jeremy persisted.

"He's all right, I suppose," she returned noncommittally over her shoulder as she continued into the kitchen.

She glimpsed the disappointment on her son's face as he returned his attention to the computer.

We're doing just fine on our own, she assured herself again as the kitchen door closed behind her. She was hanging her coat on a peg when she heard someone entering behind her. Glancing over her shoulder, she saw it was Sarah.

Resting her hands on her hips, Sarah studied her niece narrowly. "You might be able to fool your son, but you can't fool me. You streaked through the living room like a woman running for shelter."

"It's cold out there. I merely wanted to hang up my coat and get a cup of hot coffee," Irene replied. The thought of coffee made her already-knotted stomach churn, still she forced herself to put action to her words.

Sarah raised an eyebrow as if to say she wasn't buying that story. "You look as pale as a sheet. Are you going to tell me what happened or am I going to have to pry it out of you?"

Reaching for a cup, Irene realized her hands were shaking. "Murdock kissed me," she heard herself blurting.

"Are you saying he tried to force himself on you?" Sarah demanded, immediately becoming fiercely protective. "If so he'd better not set foot on this property again or I'll call the sheriff."

Giving up the pretense of wanting coffee, Irene turned to her aunt. "He didn't force himself on me. He merely kissed me like someone who was wondering if he wanted to initiate a relationship." Just mentioning the kiss brought back the remembered feel of his lips on hers with a vividness that shook her. She could almost feel the heat of his body as if he was actually there.

"And?" Sarah demanded when Irene paused and the pause lengthened into a silence.

Irene drew a shaky breath. "It's been a long time since I was kissed, that's all."

Sarah nodded knowingly. "Bells and whistles. You heard bells and whistles."

Irene started to deny this but the words stuck in her throat. She raked a hand agitatedly through her hair. "All right. So maybe metaphorically I heard bells and whistles."

"Well?" Sarah prodded when her niece again fell silent.

"There's nothing more to tell because nothing more is going to happen," Irene replied. Tersely she repeated to her aunt what she'd already told Murdock.

"You've matured too much to ever return to the dependent young woman you were. As for being too independent, if you love him you'll find ways to compromise without giving up what's important to you. A flower properly tended, neither overly tended nor undertended, will bloom forever."

Irene frowned at her aunt. "That's just the point, I don't want anyone 'tending' me."

"I was thinking in terms of marriage," Sarah said in rebuttal. "A husband and wife should not suffocate each other but there should be a strong bond of companionship between them. And each should feel confident that when they do need someone to lean on the other one will be there."

"In theory that sounds great," Irene conceded. "But theory and reality are sometimes miles apart."

"You did inherit the Orman stubbornness," Sarah said with a sigh. "But I do have one last thought I'd like you to mull over. It is my opinion that the real art of survival is first learning to stand alone and then learning that it's all right to lean on someone else at times."

"A part of me tells me you could be right," Irene admitted. "But I feel safer standing alone."

"But are you truly happy?" Sarah asked gently.

"I was. At least I was satisfied with my life," Irene replied, then realizing what she'd just said, her jaw firmed. "I am satisfied with my life," she declared firmly.

"For someone who's supposed to be so pleased with her existence, you still look pretty shaken," Sarah observed.

"I'm just tired." Irene forced a yawn. "I think I'll tuck Jeremy in and go to bed."

She found Jeremy still playing on the computer. "Mr. Parnell is pretty good at computer games," he informed her when she came to stand beside him. Again hopefulness showed in his eyes. "He really is very nice."

"I'm sure he is," she replied, keeping an indifference in her voice.

Again Jeremy looked disappointed at her lack of enthusiasm for the man. "I'll bet if you got to know him better, you'd really like him."

"I'm not interested in getting to know him better," she said firmly.

For a moment Jeremy looked as if he was going to persist, then with an expression of acceptance, he turned back to the computer screen. "I guess it's time for me to save this game and go to bed."

"You guess right," she confirmed.

"It would be nice to have another man around, though," he added abruptly, as he turned off the machine.

Irene made no comment but later as she lay in her bed she wished she'd insisted that Sarah use her bed and let her sleep on the converter sofa in the living room. The loneliness she'd felt the night before returned, only this time it was more intense. Murdock's image taunted her. She reminded herself of the difficult, anxiety-filled days following Jack's death. Still Murdock's image lingered.

Chapter Seven

"He'll probably pretend I'm not even there," Irene muttered to herself. It was midmorning. She'd slept badly. Murdock had wandered through her dreams and she'd woken feeling frustrated and restless. Now she was on her way to the Brockman place to split more firewood into kindling. She'd split a lot the other day. He probably didn't need anymore. The firewood, she admitted, was merely an excuse.

In an attempt to calm her growing nervousness, she drew a deep breath of the crisp morning air. It didn't help and her steps faltered. For a moment she considered turning back. Grimly she forced herself to proceed forward. She knew she owed Murdock an apology for the childish way she'd behaved when he offered her a ride home last night. That was one reason for this foray. She was also certain from that final look of disapproval on his face that he'd crossed her off his list of females he might be interested in pursuing. A cold-shoulder treatment from him should put him out of her dreams and let her get back to her life as it was before he arrived, she added as another reason for this expedition.

However, she wasn't feeling brave enough to seek him out to offer the apology. That would only be given if they crossed paths. She knew he was at the house. She'd seen him returning to the dock from his early-morning fishing trip a while ago. And, from her bedroom window, she'd seen him on the Brockmans' porch just moments before she'd left her house.

It might even be best if he avoided her altogether and she never did apologize, she thought as she stopped at the storage shed to pick up the equipment she would need. Keeping an animosity between them should aid in dampening the unwanted emotions he was stirring in her.

She had begun to build a small pile of kindling when she felt someone watching her. Before she even looked up, she knew he was there. Glancing toward the porch she saw him leaning against one of the posts holding up the roof, a disdainful expression on his face. But even his frosty gaze did not stop the sight of him from sending a heat rushing through her.

To give herself time to regain her cool composure, she picked up the two pieces of newly split log and tossed them into the wheelbarrow with the others. Then turning to face him, she met his gaze levelly.

But before she could speak, he held up his hands as if warding off an attack. "Don't worry, I'm not going to offer to help," he said curtly. "You seem to enjoy playing the macho heroine so go right ahead." Straightening away from the post, he started to go back inside.

Let him go. It's safer that way, her inner voice advised. But she couldn't. "I owe you an apology. I behaved childishly last night when you offered me a ride. It was cold and I do appreciate your kindness."

Mentally Irene breathed a sigh of relief. There she'd said it, now she could split a couple more pieces of wood and leave. Without waiting for his reaction, she returned her attention to the woodpile, picked up a log and split it. But as she bent to retrieve the pieces, a pair of hiking boots moved into her line of vision. As she straightened into a standing position, her gaze traveled along a pair of sturdy, jean-clad legs then upward over a heavy fleece-lined jacket until she found herself looking into Murdock's shuttered brown eyes.

"And I owe you a thank-you," he said, his expression still cool. "Having you around has eased my nightmares."

In spite of his frosty delivery, Irene experienced a glow of pleasure. "Really?"

He frowned as if angry with himself. "You've replaced them with frustration. I figure you're about as easy to get along with as a mule but I can't stop myself from wondering if I'm wrong."

Irene told herself she should be insulted but the truth was she couldn't fault him. "You could be right about the mule analogy," she admitted.

He nodded as if he was sure he was. The scowl of self-directed impatience still on his face, he again started to leave.

"How would you like to go to a movie with me, anyway?" Irene gasped. She couldn't believe those words had issued from her mouth. She'd asked him for a date. One moment she'd been wondering what it would be like to have a date with him and in the next she'd actually asked him for one.

Her heart began to pound frantically as he turned back to her. Don't panic, he won't accept, she assured herself. Reading the shock on his face, she felt like a fool. "Forget I said that," she requested stiffly.

He raised a reproving eyebrow. "Didn't your mother teach you that it's impolite to retract an invitation?"

"My mother also taught me women shouldn't ask men out," she returned, still wondering what insanity had taken hold of her.

"Apparently neither lesson stuck." Challenge showed in his eyes. "I'll pick you up at six."

She'd look as though she was running scared if she backed out now and running scared was exactly what she felt like doing, she admitted. But instead, she heard herself saying with surprising calmness, "The first showing is at seven. Pick me up at six-thirty."

"How about, if I pick you up at six. Dinner will be on me. Then we'll go to the second showing," he suggested.

The image of them sharing an intimate meal across a candlelit table caused a warm curl of excitement. Even just the thought of sitting with him in a booth at the local diner suddenly made the diner seem like a romantic spot. Her resistance to him was much too low, she moaned silently. "The invitation was for a movie, that's all," she said firmly.

As this declaration hung in the air between them, Irene suddenly remembered Sarah and Jeremy. This date would be as much of a shock to them as it still was to her. She could easily picture her aunt greeting Murdock with excessive enthusiasm and Jeremy smiling hopefully up at the man as if they saw him as the answer to their prayers. "And, I'll pick you up. I'm the one who did the asking."

A dark cloud of impatience seemed to pass over his face and she was certain he was reconsidering his decision to accept her invitation. "Six-thirty it is," he said curtly, then strode inside.

Irene watched him depart in a stunned silence. She'd been sure he was going to call the whole thing off.

"Going out with him could turn out to be a good thing," she told herself as she returned to splitting wood. They probably had dissimilar tastes. After all, she guessed he lived a fairly cosmopolitan life and she was merely a country girl. "No doubt we'll get on each other's nerves immediately."

Feeling a prickling on her neck, she glanced covertly at the house as she tossed a freshly cut piece of wood on the pile she was building. Murdock was watching her from the window. "In fact he's already getting on my nerves," she muttered, the prickling sensation moving lower to cause an uncomfortable tightening between her shoulder blades.

Deciding it was time to go, she picked up her tools and headed back to the shed.

Murdock was fully aware of the grim expression on Irene Galvin's face as she rounded the house on her way home. Going out with her was not only going to be uncomfortable, but most likely the worst date he'd ever had. He'd heard her gasp and seen the stunned look in her eyes when she realized she'd asked him out. And he knew he'd trapped her into keeping the invitation open. But he needed to get this woman out of his mind, and if spending one long painful evening with her would do the trick then he was willing to go through with it.

That evening as she drove to the Brockman place, Irene congratulated herself on her quick thinking earlier that day when she'd insisted on picking up Murdock. The guilt she'd felt about asking her aunt to baby-sit had been quickly washed away by Sarah's delight at the prospect of Irene having a date with the man. In fact, both Sarah and Jeremy had been even more enthusiastic than she'd imagined they would be. Having Murdock pick her up might have been a truly embarrassing experience.

Pulling up in front of the Brockman place, she waited for him to come out. A minute passed and her already taut nerves grew even tauter. Two minutes passed.

Maybe he'd changed his mind about going out on the date, she thought hopefully. But if he had, she was sure he would have called. Maybe he'd had an accident and was lying inside unconscious or hurt. This thought brought a surge of anxiety. Turning off her engine, she climbed out of the car and mounted the steps to the porch.

Reaching the door, prudence demanded that she knock before simply bursting into the house. It could be that he'd simply forgotten about the time and was running late, she cautioned herself. She rapped loudly.

Almost immediately the door was opened.

Murdock was wearing slacks, a designer turtleneck shirt and carrying a sport coat. Obviously he'd chosen to treat this date as the real thing, she mused, glad she'd chosen a pair of corduroy slacks and a sweater instead of simply remaining in her jeans. And he'd freshly shaved, she realized as a light whiff of spicy after-shave reached her. Nice scent, she thought as the masculine fragrance teased her nostrils enticingly.

Fighting to quell the increasing attraction she was feeling, she said accusingly, "When you didn't come out, I thought you might have fallen and hurt yourself."

"My mother taught me that a man should always go to the door to collect a lady for a date. It seemed to me that turnabout was only fair play."

Irene met his gaze. If he was making fun of her then this date was over here and now, she promised herself. But there was no mockery in those dark eyes of his. There was, however, challenge as if he expected her, at any moment, to flee. The thought that maybe that action would be the smartest crossed her mind. But pride and the question of how she would explain her retreat to Jeremy and Sarah stopped her.

Two can play this game, she told herself. "Your mother was right." Challenge now flickered in her eyes. "May I help you with your coat?"

For a moment he looked as if he was going to refuse, then abruptly he grinned impishly. "If you insist."

Her heart skipped a beat at his unexpected playfulness. Taking his coat from him, she held it for him. *Big mistake,* her inner voice scolded her. Just the lightest brush of her fingertips against his shirt was sending charged currents of excitement racing through her. Again she was aware of the strength of his shoulders and the firm build of his arms. The way his thick dark hair was a touch too long for his conservative hairstyle so that it curled just slightly at the ends along his neck held her attention and she found herself wanting to run her fingers through it.

Stop thinking thoughts like that! she ordered herself and quickly finished assisting him with his coat. Opening the door, she stepped aside to allow him to exit ahead of her. "Shall we get going," she said with command.

Nodding he stepped outside. As she joined him, he paused to throw the bolt. She waited until the door was locked, then with a wave of her hand, indicated she expected him to precede her to the car. The impish grin returned and he complied. But when she opened the car door for him, she saw him hesitate as if he thought she was carrying her macho behavior a little too far. Then he shrugged and climbed in.

"There's only a choice between two movies," she said as she guided the car toward the main road. She named them. One was a comedy and the other an action film.

"You choose," he replied.

"I'd prefer the action one," she replied, honestly.

He smiled with relief. "Good choice."

That they both had the same taste in movies bothered her a little. She was looking for reasons they would never get along. "Nice evening," he said, breaking the silence that had fallen between them.

"Yeah," she agreed. "Nice and clear." Silently she groaned. They'd both used the word "nice." That was definitely a sign this wasn't going well. In the next instant, she drew a mental breath of relief. That was exactly what she wanted. "We could use some rain," she said in a more relaxed voice, now certain this date was going to work out the way she'd hoped.

"I guess when it's too dry, you do have to worry about forest fires," he said thoughtfully, his gaze traveling over the heavily wooded landscape.

Irene nodded.

"Have you ever considered living someplace else?"

Surprised by the question, Irene glanced at him but there was only casual interest on his face. "I love it here, but I'm not rooted here," she replied truthfully. "Aunt Sarah is always reminding me that variety is the spice of life. And I like to think that if an opportunity for a change that would benefit Jeremy and myself came along, I wouldn't be so stuck in a rut I wouldn't take it."

"You're not quite as set in your ways as I was beginning to think."

"How very cavalier of you to say that," she returned dryly. Still, the note of approval she'd heard in his voice brought a light flush of pleasure to her cheeks.

A few minutes later as they parked on Main Street in front of the movie theater, she wondered if he expected her to come around and open his door. As if in answer, the moment she removed her keys from the ignition, he opened his own door and climbed out. Clearly, while he actually seemed to enjoy letting her play the role of the macho partner while they were in private, he wanted no public display. As they entered the theater, she wondered if he was going to object to her paying. She'd already made up her mind that since she'd asked him on this date, buying the tickets was her responsibility.

"Evening, Irene," Sheryl Springer greeted her from behind the combined ticket and concession counter. Irene had known the pretty, voluptuous redhead all her life. Sheryl was in her mid-twenties and had a steady boyfriend. Even so, Irene noticed that although the redhead was speaking to her, Sheryl's eyes never left Murdock. The same "she'd better keep her hands off my man" feeling Irene had experienced when a woman had looked at Jack that way stirred within her. He is not *my man,* she scolded herself curtly.

Irene named the movie they'd chosen and asked for two tickets. As she pulled the money out of her wallet, she saw Murdock shove his hands into the pockets of his slacks. A glance at his face let her see the shadow of discomfort this was causing him, then his expression became shuttered. Feeling as if she might have carried this macho business too far, she said as she accepted her change, "I lost a bet."

Sheryl smiled sweetly at Murdock. "I wouldn't mind losing whatever that bet was."

A few minutes later as they sat eating popcorn and waiting for the show to start, Murdock cast her a dour look. "Would you mind explaining that business about the bet?" he demanded in a gruff whisper near her ear.

She frowned at the tone of reprimand in his voice. "You looked as if my paying was bruising your male ego. I was merely attempting to come up with a way to save face for you." His warm breath playing against her neck was causing her to feel slightly giddy. An unexpected burst of mischief caused her to add, "You wouldn't want her to think you were so desperate for a date, you'd go out with any woman who asked?"

Abruptly he grinned. "I think I'd be more flattered if she thought I was a male demimonde."

Irene cast him a dubious glance. "A what?"

"A gigolo whose services are eagerly sought by wealthy women," he elaborated, laughter glistening in his eyes.

She grinned back at him. "I like a man with a sense of humor."

He regarded her with mock indignation. "Are you saying you think I might die of starvation if I should attempt to live off my manly wiles?"

"Well, I suppose I shouldn't jump to any conclusion. They say you can't always judge a book by its cover," she said, bantering back. Silently she gulped. That was definitely salacious flirting. In fact, she sounded like a woman who might be seriously seeking a man. Which I am not! she reminded herself firmly.

Surprise showed in Murdock's eyes. It was quickly replaced by an exaggerated licentious expression. "Some people claim they've experienced some of life's truly exciting moments between the covers—" he smiled mischievously and paused momentarily before adding "—of a book."

The double entendre was delivered too obviously to miss. The loneliness she'd been experiencing these past few nights descended over Irene. Fun and adventure, she thought wistfully, as memories of times spent between the sheets with Jack flooded her mind. Abruptly she stiffened. The man she was suddenly picturing herself with wasn't Jack. It was Murdock.

To her relief the lights dimmed at that moment and previews of coming attractions began playing on the screen. Frantically she tried to conjure up a sharp image of Jack.

Her memories of him were enough to last her a lifetime, she assured herself. But just as she was bringing Jack into sharp focus, Murdock's shoulder brushed against hers. A heat raced down her arm and the man beside her claimed her full attention.

Admitting that memories were no protection against her body's traitorous responses to Murdock, she ordered herself to concentrate on the movie. This method of trying to vanquish the man beside her from her mind was almost working when he leaned toward her and said something in her ear.

Vaguely her brain registered the fact that he'd made a comment about the car chase but his closeness made thinking difficult. She managed a quiet, "Uh-huh," as she fought down the urge to shift just enough so that her shoulder was resting against his. This desire for physical contact shook her and she huddled more securely into her own chair.

Glancing toward him, she found herself thinking he could very easily become a wealthy gigolo if he ever decided to pursue that occupation.

By the time the movie was over, Irene's nerves were near the breaking point. Her hope that spending an evening with Murdock would help her fight her attraction for the man was gone.

"How about allowing me to salvage my male ego by letting me treat you to coffee and dessert?" he suggested as they climbed back into her car.

Just the thought of sitting across a table from him, with him constantly in her line of vision caused her to feel weak. "I'm really tired," she replied stiffly. "I think we should go straight home." Without giving him a chance to argue, she guided the car out of town.

A silence hung between them as she drove. The fact that he wasn't even trying to make small talk about the movie

convinced her that she would never have to worry about him
asking her out on a date. Which was exactly what she
wanted, she affirmed. Expecting to see boredom etched into
his features, she glanced covertly at him. His hands were
clasped behind his head and his expression shuttered as he
sat leaning back staring out the windshield. He seemed
oblivious to her presence. He's probably mentally building
a new computer system to pass the time until I get him
home, she decided.

Pulling up in front of the Brockman house, she half expected him to be out of the car and on his way up the steps
before she even shifted into Park. Instead he remained
seated, his hands still clasped behind his head in a relaxed
pose. For a moment she thought he'd fallen asleep, then he
turned his head to look at her. "Well?" he said as if he expected something from her.

She frowned in confusion. "Well, what?"

"Well, aren't you going to escort me to my door?"

She couldn't believe he was considering playing this date
out to the end. "I figured you could find it on your own."

"Tisk. Tisk. That is not a gentlemanly attitude," he
chided.

There was a firm set to his jaw that warned her they could
be there all night if she didn't go along with the game.
"Have it your way," she said, switching off the engine.

He waited until she'd opened his door before he even
moved out of his relaxed position. "Thank you," he said
politely as he climbed out.

"You're welcome," she replied, giving the door a shove
to close it. Looking up at him, she felt emotions stirring
within her she didn't want wakened. "I'm sure you can
make it to your door on your own from here," she said,
starting back around her car.

Murdock's hand closed around her arm bringing her to a halt. "What would Miss Manners say about you leaving your date on the curb?" he admonished.

Even through the heavy thickness of her coat she could feel the heat of his touch. She had to get away from him as quickly as possible. "All right, I'll walk you to your door." She jerked her arm, attempting to free it but he held her easily.

"If you'll stop squirming so I don't have to worry about you losing your balance and falling, I'll let go," he bargained.

Scowling up at him, she stiffened and immediately was released. "Shall we?" he coaxed, motioning toward the porch steps.

"This is ridiculous," she muttered, accompanying him onto the porch.

At the door, he found his key and inserted it into the lock and turned it.

"Do I have to wait here until you're inside or can I leave now?" she asked dryly.

"First I should thank you properly."

Irene swallowed a lump of panic as his hands cupped her face. He was going to kiss her. She ordered her feet to get her out of there but they remained planted like a couple of solidly rooted oaks. "That really isn't necessary." She managed to choke out the words.

"But it is," he replied without compromise. His head lowered to hers and very gently his lips met hers.

Her heart pounded painfully against the walls of her chest as she again ordered herself to get out of there. But instead, she lifted her head to harden the kiss. Traitor! she screamed at her body as the heat of the contact pervaded every fiber of her being. Releasing her face, Murdock drew her into his embrace. Unable to stop herself, her arms circled his shoulders.

"You do taste good," he murmured against her lips.

Tremors of delight raced through her. "And you taste like popcorn," she murmured back. "Popcorn has always been one of my favorite foods."

She felt him smile. Then his mouth left hers to trail kisses around to the sensitive hollow behind her ear.

A blaze as intense as any she'd ever felt ignited within her. And when he nibbled on her earlobe, she could barely get her breath. Panic suddenly filled her. Frantically, she pushed him away. "No," she gasped.

For a long moment, he stood looking down at her in silence, then he said calmly, "We need to talk."

"No, we don't need to talk," she returned, the fear of the emotions he'd aroused increasing by the second. Afraid she might not be able to resist him if she stayed, she started down the steps.

Murdock's hand closed around her arm once again, bringing her to a halt. "Who are you running away from, Irene? Me or yourself?" he asked gruffly.

"Both," she admitted, attempting to pull free.

Carefully, so she wouldn't lose her balance, he released her. "Running away never solves anything," he cautioned.

"But it can prevent a lot of pain," she blurted. Embarrassed and totally shaken by her openness, she turned away from him and strode to her car.

Murdock stood on the porch and watched her drive away. When a woman's mind is set, it takes a miracle to change it, he warned himself. Still, the taste of her lips lingered on his.

"You're home early," Sarah observed as Irene entered the living room on her way to her bedroom.

"We just went to the early movie, that was all," Irene replied.

Sarah had been lying, relaxed in the sofa bed reading a magazine. Now she sat up straight and her gaze narrowed on her niece. "You look shaken."

"It's been a long time since I've dated. The experience conjured up old memories," Irene hedged.

"Are you sure it's the old memories that are bothering you?" Sarah questioned.

Irene drew a terse breath. "Murdock stirred up some emotions I don't want stirred up ever again."

Sarah regarded her knowingly. "You like him a lot, don't you? I can almost feel the sparks flying between the two of you."

"They might be flying but they are not going to land and start a fire," Irene said firmly.

"Sometimes the heart has a mind of its own," Sarah cautioned.

"Well, mine is going to behave and do what I say," Irene declared. Then wishing her aunt a good-night, she went up to her room.

Alone in the darkness, tears brimmed in her eyes. She was never going to fall in love again. *Never,* she promised herself as she escaped into the dark abyss of sleep.

Chapter Eight

Irene walked slowly back to the house. It was still early morning. When Jeremy had come downstairs for breakfast, she'd managed to field his questions about her date without sounding either unfriendly toward Murdock or giving the impression she and Murdock were now friends.

But her son could be persistent and the hopefulness in his eyes had caused a part of her to want to give in to the feelings she was having for the man. Before her nerves could snap, she'd left Sarah preparing pancakes for Jeremy and escaped using the excuse of retrieving the newspaper. The paper box along with the mailbox was at the end of their private road a little over half a mile from the house. Maintaining a leisurely pace, she calculated that by the time she got back, Jeremy would have only a short while before he had to leave for school and Sarah had volunteered to drive him again today.

"And that will give me some time alone," she murmured gratefully. A frigid breeze whirled around her and she hugged her coat more tightly to her to ward off a chill. The warmth of Murdock's touch suddenly filled her mind and her hands balled into fists. "I am not falling in love with him," she stated firmly as if speaking the words aloud would make them so.

A salvaging thought abruptly occurred to her and a look of relief spread over her face. "I *really* am not falling in love with him," she said, this time with true conviction. "What I'm experiencing is simply physical attraction. I'm still young and it's been a long time since I've been intimate with a man. He's attractive. It's only natural my hormones would be stimulated." Pleased with herself for discovering this reasonable explanation for the emotional turmoil brewing within, she actually relaxed as she mounted the steps to her back porch.

But as she entered her kitchen, her muscles tensed so violently, she experienced a sharp jab of pain in her back. Seated at her table, eating breakfast with her son and Sarah, was Murdock Parnell.

"Jeremy invited me in for pancakes," he said, smiling a greeting at her. "I'd never had them made with cranberries." His gaze leveled on her. "I couldn't resist the temptation."

He was talking about her. She read that in his eyes. A fire sparked within her while panic threatened to overwhelm her. "There are some temptations it's best to avoid," she cautioned, as much to herself as to him.

"Aunt Sarah's pancakes aren't that bad." Jeremy quickly spoke up in Sarah's defense.

"No, of course not," Irene agreed, forcing a smile as she turned to her son.

Sarah's gaze traveled from Murdock to Irene. There was a knowing look in her eyes that told Irene her aunt had guessed that pancakes weren't really the subject under discussion. Sarah's attention shifted to Jeremy. "Time for us to be leaving so I can get you to school on time."

Jeremy looked reluctant to leave Murdock. "You want to come along and see my school?" he asked.

"Maybe tomorrow," Murdock replied in an easy drawl.

Jeremy beamed with anticipation as if taking this as a promise and raced out of the room to fetch his book bag.

"You stay and finish your pancakes," Sarah ordered Murdock as she rose from the table and went to the stove. After scooping up two more from a covered platter onto a fresh plate, she set that plate across from him. "And you eat yours while they're still hot," she ordered Irene.

Jeremy came racing back in before Irene could form a protest. He gave his mother a hug, Murdock a high five, grabbed his coat and hurried out the back door.

Taking up her purse and coat and following him, Sarah paused in the doorway to glance back at Irene. "Eat!" she commanded. "A healthy breakfast is the beginning of a happy day, especially when there's a good-looking man sitting across your breakfast table."

Irene raised an eyebrow to let her aunt know she realized she was being maneuvered. But I'm not that easily manipulated, she added silently.

"You should eat these while they're hot," Murdock said. "They're very tasty."

Her gaze shifted to him. The thought that seeing him at her breakfast table every morning would be a pleasant sight, flashed through her mind. Self-directed anger swept though her and brought an iciness to her eyes. "I thought I made it clear last night I didn't want to see you on a personal basis."

Murdock's polite mask fell away. "You did and, believe me, I spent a restless night debating about bowing to your wishes." He rose. Squaring his shoulders, he faced her grimly. "My grandfather told me he saw my grandmother across a dance floor and knew she was the one for him. My father claimed the first time he saw my mother smile, he knew she was the only woman for him. I always figured they were both romanticizing, at least a little. After you came into my life, I hoped they were."

Irene's nerves tensed. She didn't want to hear what he was saying. Her protective shield was much too fragile. "I'm sure they were. And I've got chores to do," she said, heading for the door to the living room.

In two long strides, Murdock blocked her retreat. "In the best of all worlds, I imagined meeting the woman I wanted for my wife and both of us instantly knowing we were meant for each other. The more practical side of me figured I'd meet someone I was attracted to, we'd date, get to know each other, become friends and realize we were in love. You don't fit into either of those scenarios."

"I'm sure you'll find someone who will." As Irene spoke, her words seemed to twist like a knife inside her. Her shield cracked dangerously. She had to get out of there. Turning she headed for the outside door.

"First I have to convince myself I'd be a fool to stick around here and try to change your mind," he said gruffly.

His hand closed around her arm, again stopping her retreat. "I've thought a lot about that kiss last night and the one before that. I don't claim to be an expert on women but I was sure you enjoyed both of them."

She knew lying would only make her appear foolish. "You kiss nicely and it's been a long time since I've been kissed by an available male."

He grinned crookedly. "That's a start."

"No, it's a finish," she replied firmly.

His frown returned. "I swear to you I won't try to shackle your independence. The truth is I need a wife who can fend for herself. My job requires traveling. Sometimes I'll be able to take my family with me and other times I won't.''

She knew he was being truthful. But instead of relief, her tension increased. A deeply buried pain had begun to bubble to the surface and she was forced to admit that her fear of becoming dependent had only been a sham to hide the true anguish that haunted her. ''Then I wish you luck in finding a woman who meets your requirements.''

Challenge flickered in his eyes. ''Are you sure you don't want to be that woman?''

Again his nearness was playing havoc with her senses. Her blood raced, her heart pounded and she found herself wanting him to stop talking and kiss her. ''No.'' The word blurted out, more a command to herself than to him. ''Now, will you please release me,'' she demanded, fighting to maintain control over the panic rising within her.

''That's not the request I saw in your eyes,'' he said softly, reaching up and stroking her cheek.

Her jaw trembled and the desire to be held by him filled her. Don't give in to this, her inner voice wailed.

He bent his head toward hers. She knew he was going to kiss her. Run! she ordered herself. Then his lips found hers. Fire swept through her. She wanted to melt into his arms.

Suddenly memories of Jack's funeral were overwhelming her. Tears began streaming down her cheeks.

''Irene?'' Stopping the kiss and releasing her, Murdock stared at her in stunned surprise.

''I will not go through that loss again,'' she sobbed. Brushing at her tears, she glared up at him. ''I refuse to fall in love again. When Jack died I felt as if a part of me had been ripped out. But somehow I healed. I won't allow myself to be hurt like that again.''

For a long moment Murdock studied her in silence. "Taking the chance of suffering that kind of hurt is part of life," he said at last.

"It's not going to be a part of my life," she returned defiantly. "I'm happy just the way I am and that's how I'm going to stay."

He traced the line of her jaw. "Are you really willing to settle for what you have?"

"Yes." In spite of the conviction in her voice, Irene felt herself weakening. A part of her wanted to be in his arms but the remembered pain was too strong. A fresh flood of hot tears burned behind her eyes. Afraid they would spill over, she gestured toward the door. "Would you please leave."

Murdock looked as if he was going to argue, then with a shrug, he said, "Eat your pancakes," and left.

Her home seemed suddenly cold and empty. The urge to run after him was nearly overpowering. She forced herself to again relive the agony of Jack's funeral. The pain had been so unbearable, she'd hardly been able to breathe. Only the thought that she had a small son who needed her had kept her from wallowing in a sea of despair. "I can't go through that again," she repeated weakly as the tears she'd been holding back escaped and flowed down her cheeks.

Murdock frowned as he climbed back into Horace's boat and guided it across the lake. First the earthquake and now Irene Galvin. "My dad told me life would be rough at times," he muttered. However, he'd never let adversity deter him in the past and he wasn't going to give up without a fight this time. "I just hope that stubborn streak in her doesn't reach all the way to the core," he added.

"Well?"

Irene looked over her shoulder to see her aunt entering the

room. "Well, what?" she asked with schooled indifference. Sarah frowned impatiently. "How did breakfast go?"

"The pancakes were delicious," Irene lied. She hadn't been able to force herself to eat a single bite. The lump in her throat had been too big. Instead she'd busied herself doing laundry and cleaning the kitchen. Concentrating on those activities, she'd managed to get the lump swallowed. Now she was ironing and watching the news on television. And determinedly not thinking about Murdock.

"I'm not asking about the pancakes. I want to know about how you and Murdock got along," Sarah demanded insistently.

Like a floodgate opening, the exchange between her and Murdock flowed uncontrolled into Irene's mind, blocking out everything else. Unable to think of an artful dodge, she said bluntly, "He mentioned something about him thinking I was the woman he wanted to marry and I told him I wasn't interested in falling in love again. I asked him to leave and he left."

For a moment Sarah regarded her niece in stunned silence, then she frowned reprovingly. "He said he was interested in marrying you and you just tossed him out? Don't you think you're carrying this independence thing a bit too far? You could have at least given yourself time to get to know him."

Irene recalled how easily Murdock could crack the barrier she kept around herself. "No, I couldn't."

"I cannot believe you've become so closed-minded you won't even allow yourself to indulge in a little romance," Sarah scolded.

The remembered feel of Murdock's lips tormented Irene. "You don't understand!" she said through clenched teeth.

Sarah's expression softened. "What don't I understand?" she prodded gently.

"A little romance could lead to me falling in love with Murdock Parnell," Irene confessed, unable to hold this truth in. She met her aunt's gaze. "After Jack died I promised myself I would never have to go through that kind of loss again."

Sarah nodded understandingly. "So that's the real reason behind your determination to remain alone. I did find your argument for independence a little weak. You're much too strong a woman now to feel threatened that anyone could truly rule over you. I guessed there was something else holding you back."

"Well, now you know," Irene said tiredly. "And I hope you'll respect my wishes and there will be no more mention of Murdock Parnell or marriage or romance."

The look of disapproval returned to Sarah's face. "And like a frightened mouse in its hole, you'll keep that part of yourself curled tightly in a little ball and hidden away from the world?"

"That's about it," Irene replied defiantly.

"Even a frightened mouse has to come out for food or die," Sarah warned.

"I can live without a man in my life. I have you and all the rest of our family to love. And I have Jeremy. That's enough for me," Irene said with finality.

"A second chance for love like the one you have with Murdock doesn't come around often," Sarah cautioned. "If I were you, I'd give this some serious thought."

"Believe me, I have," Irene replied, then pointedly returned her attention to her ironing and the television, letting her aunt know she considered this conversation over. To her relief, Sarah acquiesced without protest.

It took willpower but for the rest of the day, Irene was able to keep Murdock mostly in the back of her mind. Every once in a while he'd manage to work his way to the forefront but she'd quickly push him back. She was, in fact, beginning to relax by the time she walked down to the main road to meet Jeremy's school bus.

"Did you like the pancakes?" her son asked as soon as the bus had driven away and they started toward home.

She could tell by the gleam in his eyes he wasn't really interested in her reaction to the pancakes but rather to her breakfast companion. Determined not to allow Murdock to become the subject of conversation, she said, "They were good." Then she quickly asked, "How was school today? Anything interesting happen?"

"Nope, nothing," he replied. He smiled up at her encouragingly. "We should ask Murdock to dinner. He's probably not eating something from all of the basic food groups like we do. You wouldn't want him to get sick."

"I'm sure he's eating just fine," she replied.

Jeremy's expression became very adult. "I really think we should invite him to dinner. He really liked Great-aunt Sarah's pancakes."

"We are not asking him to dinner," Irene said firmly. "Now tell me about school."

For a moment Jeremy looked as if he was going to persist, then shrugging he said, "There's not much to tell."

The dejected expression on his face tore at Irene's heart. Murdock will be leaving soon and a day after he's gone, Jeremy will have forgotten him, she assured herself. Well, maybe it'll take a week, she amended, forced to admit Murdock would be a hard man to forget quickly. "I was thinking that after Sarah leaves we could go visit Grandpa and Grandma Galvin for a weekend," she suggested, hoping to cheer him up.

"Yeah, sure," he replied, without the enthusiasm he usually displayed when she mentioned the prospect of a visit with his grandparents.

Irene wished her resistance to Murdock was stronger, but it wasn't. Even for her son, she couldn't risk having him around. Uncertain of what to say, she allowed a silence to fall between her and Jeremy.

"Can I go visit Mr. Parnell for a while before I do my homework?" he asked as they entered the house and he dumped his book bag on the floor beside the table.

She would have preferred to say no for her own sake. The farther she could put Murdock out of her life, the better. But that wasn't being fair to Jeremy. Besides, her son would want a reason and she was in no mood to try to explain her feelings to him. "As long as you don't invite him to dinner," she stipulated.

"I've just baked some sugar cookies," Sarah said, reminding them of her presence. "I'll bag up a few for you to take along."

As Jeremy yelled a thank-you and quickly hurried down the hall to use the bathroom before heading over to the Brockman house, Irene looked at the cookies her aunt was packaging.

"What's the secret ingredient this time?" she asked, looking for something to take her mind off of Murdock.

Sarah gave a shrug. "No secret ingredient. They're just plain old-fashioned sugar cookies," she replied.

Irene's gaze jerked to her aunt. "Plain sugar cookies?" she asked, with disbelief.

"They're not bad. In fact, they're not even dull," Sarah said, taking a bite from one as if to prove her point. A melancholy expression suddenly played across her features. "My grandma Perry, your grandma Orman's mother, used to make the best sugar cookies I've ever eaten."

Irene studied her aunt. She'd never seen her in this kind of mood before. "I vaguely remember her. When I was around six, I think, my dad decided we'd all go out to

Wyoming so my brother and I could meet our great-grandparents. You were living with them.''

Sarah grinned. ''That was just before I joined the navy. I think the whole purpose of that trip was so that your father could talk me out of my decision. But my mind was set.''

''I remember Great-grandma and Grandpa Perry lived on a ranch,'' Irene said, trying hard to recall some detail of that trip. ''It seemed to be in the middle of nowhere.''

''It was, almost,'' Sarah replied, the reminiscent look in her eyes deepening. ''But I always loved it out there. From the time I was nine, I'd spend my summers with them. I'd help with the roundup and the harvesting. They used to grow a lot of their own feed for their cattle.'' A shadow crossed her face. ''When my parents died in that boating accident, Grandma and Grandpa Perry seemed like the logical place for me to go. I was fourteen at the time. Your uncle Prescott, he was the next youngest, was already in the navy. Your aunt Belinda had married John Hanks and they were off in a Brazilian jungle studying plant life. Maude was down in Texas living on her own. She couldn't afford to take me in. Your dad and mom were just starting their own family. I figured they didn't need another mouth to feed. And Lester, Eloise's father, was having marital problems. Besides, grandma and grandpa Perry were getting on in years. They needed me as much as I needed them.''

Sarah frowned. ''I haven't been back to Wyoming for years. After my grandparents both died and Uncle Orville took over the ranch, I visited a couple of times, but it wasn't the same.'' Abruptly she shook her shoulders. The frown became a self-conscious smile. ''I don't know what's got me to thinking about Wyoming again.''

''Sometimes old memories are the best,'' Irene suggested, wishing she could escape into the past and put Murdock Parnell out of her mind.

Sarah's jaw firmed. "No. Old memories can give moments of pleasant reminiscence but a person cannot live in the past." She regarded Irene pointedly. "One has to get on with one's life."

Irene groaned silently. Sarah had managed to turn the conversation back to her. "I am," she stated. Then before Sarah could again mention Murdock, she quickly left.

Murdock was sitting on the porch with his feet propped up on the rail when Jeremy joined him. The breeze was crisp but the sun was hot.

"Sarah sent these cookies," Jeremy said, handing Murdock the bag before seating himself and propping his legs up in an imitation of the man.

"And what do we have today?" Murdock asked with a grin. "Olive and peanut butter? Or maybe she's incorporated onion and garlic into chocolate chips."

"No. They're just plain sugar cookies." Jeremy smiled encouragingly. "But they're not bland. They're real good."

Taking one out of the bag Murdock examined it. "Are you sure she didn't add some secret ingredient she's wondering if we can detect?"

Excitement glistened in Jeremy's eyes. "Maybe."

Murdock took a bite. "Well, if there is one, I can't taste it," he admitted as he finished swallowing the morsel. He took a second bite. "These are good."

Jeremy nodded in agreement. A look of embarrassment spread over his face. "Aunt Sarah asked me to give you a message."

The hesitation in the boy's voice made Murdock uneasy. He'd hoped to have Sarah on his side and he'd thought she was. Now suddenly he was worried that Irene had convinced her aunt she was better off alone. "And what is the message?" he coaxed when Jeremy's pause continued to lengthen.

"She said I was supposed to tell you she hoped you weren't a quitter," the boy said in a rush. Immediately he added, "I told her I knew you weren't but she insisted I was supposed to say that to you."

Murdock drew a breath of relief as he reached over and ruffled the boy's hair to let him know he wasn't offended by Sarah's admonition. "You can tell her that I'm not a quitter," he said firmly.

Jeremy smiled broadly. "I knew that." His embarrassment gone, curiosity now glistened in his eyes. "What is it aunt Sarah doesn't want you to be a quitter about?"

"You remember those sparks between men and women we talked about?" Murdock asked.

Jeremy nodded.

"Well, I got hit by a few," Murdock admitted, then added bluntly, "I'd like to marry your mom."

Jeremy issued a triumphant, "Yes!" followed by "That's great. We'll make a terrific family. You can teach me more about computers and I can teach you about fishing."

The boy's enthusiasm warmed Murdock's heart. But his sense of fair play forced its way to the forefront. He wanted Irene to marry him because she wanted to, not because she'd been pressured into it by her son and aunt. "I don't want you saying anything about this to your mom. She has to be allowed to make up her own mind."

Jeremy grimaced unhappily at this stipulation.

"I want your promise," Murdock insisted.

With a disgruntled expression, Jeremy extended his hand. "I promise."

Murdock accepted the handshake and offered him a cookie.

Sitting back in his chair, Jeremy took a bite, swallowed, then turned to Murdock. "My mom can be real hard-headed," he warned.

Murdock nodded. "I've learned that."

"But I'm sure you can get her to change her mind," the boy added with conviction.

"I appreciate your confidence in me," Murdock replied.

Jeremy's mouth formed a firm line. "We men have to stick together."

"Yep," Murdock agreed. Glancing at the boy, he realized how totally comfortable he felt with him. It was as if a bond had been forged between them. Now all he had to do was convince Irene Galvin he was someone she needed permanently in her life.

Chapter Nine

Pretending to be absorbed in doing the crossword in the evening paper, Irene studied her son covertly. When he'd returned from visiting with Murdock, he'd made a point of coming into the kitchen and telling Sarah how much Murdock had enjoyed the cookies. Catching his mother's eye he'd added, "He's really a great guy."

Irene had managed a stiff smile while issuing a mental groan. She wasn't in any mood to listen to her son sing Murdock's praises all evening. Then another thought struck her. Had Murdock enlisted her son's aid in trying to break down her defenses? In the next instant, a light of hope glowed. If he had, that would be a tremendous help in keeping her barriers up. She could never respect a man who would use a child for coercion. But after the one pointed observation, Jeremy hadn't mentioned Murdock again. And now he was smiling while doing his homework.

Shifting her attention to her aunt, she discovered Sarah sitting as still as a statue, her knitting lying idle in her lap while she stared fixedly into the fire gently burning on the grate. "Sarah, is something wrong?' she asked with concern.

Sarah shook her shoulders as if breaking away from the thoughts that had been holding her captive. "Watching you allowing the past to control your destiny has made me think about my own life," she replied. "Maybe there are some ghosts I need to exorcise."

"Do you want to talk about them?" Irene asked gently.

Sarah smiled crookedly. "I think maybe these are ones I need to face rather than talk about."

A knock on the door stopped Irene from probing further. Rising to answer it, she noticed Jeremy looking her way. Immediately he returned his attention to his books but not before she saw the excited expectation on his face. Suspicion blossomed. "Jeremy, did you ask Mr. Parnell to come by this evening?" she asked curtly.

With the proud expression of someone wrongly accused of a misdeed, he met her gaze. "You told me not to and I didn't."

The knock sounded again.

"Shouldn't you be answering that?" Sarah suggested. "It is chilly out there tonight."

Assuring herself that after her encounter with Murdock this morning, the man would not be on her doorstep this evening, Irene continued to the door. Opening it, she fought to hold back a gasp. She'd been wrong. Murdock was there. His coat was unbuttoned and she could see he was dressed in a suit. In one hand he held a huge bouquet of flowers and in the other a box of candy.

"Aren't you going to invite me in?" he asked when she simply stood staring at him.

Just the sight of him was causing her heart to beat faster. "What are you doing here?" she demanded, furious with herself for wanting to be in his arms and angry with him for disobeying her request that he stay out of her life.

"I've come courting," he replied.

"Ask the man in," Sarah ordered from her seat by the fire. "I'm sure your mother taught you some manners."

"Evening, Sarah." Murdock smiled warmly over Irene's shoulder. Glancing in Jeremy's direction, he winked comradely. "How's the schoolwork coming?"

"I'm just about done," Jeremy replied, grinning happily.

"I thought I made it clear this morning, I wasn't interested in being courted," Irene said through clenched teeth, glaring accusingly at Murdock as he returned his attention to her.

"You're letting a lot of cold air in," he cautioned, taking a step forward into the room without waiting for her formal invitation.

She stepped back hurriedly to avoid contact and saw the hint of a frown at the corner of his mouth. Then again only politeness showed on his face as he gave the door a nudge with his foot and sent it closing behind him.

Before Irene could offer another protest, he extended the bouquet of flowers and the candy toward her. "For you," he said.

She clasped her hands behind her. "I don't want them," she snapped in hushed tones that would not carry to her son or Sarah.

A sudden spark of amusement showed in his eyes. Following her lead, he leaned closer to her and, keeping his voice low so that only she could hear him, he said, "The last time I saw a look like that it was on my six-year-old niece Katie's face. Her mother wanted her to eat brussels sprouts. The vegetables were good for her and I could be very good for you if you'd give me a chance."

Irene flushed with embarrassment at the comparison between her and his niece. He was right. She was behaving like a child. Not only that, but she had an audience. However, she added to herself, unlike the brussels sprouts being good for his niece, he was not good for her. Unclasping her hands, she forced a polite smile. "The flowers are beautiful and I'm sure the candy will be delicious," she said stiffly, accepting the gifts.

"And now you're supposed to ask me to sit down," he prompted.

An avenue of escape occurred to her. Her smile became more genuine. "Please, have a seat in front of the fire. I'll just go put these flowers in some water."

A shadow of disgruntlement crossed Murdock's brow and she knew he'd guessed her ploy and didn't have a counter.

"Are you going to open the candy?" Jeremy asked.

She glanced at her son to see him eyeing the box with interest. Bless that sweet tooth of his, she thought recognizing a further opportunity to assure diverting Murdock's attention from her. Turning to Jeremy, she extended the box in his direction. "Here, you can open it and share it with Mr. Parnell and your aunt while I take care of the flowers."

She almost lost her grip on both the flowers and the box as Murdock eased her hair back behind her ear with a finger then, again leaning down to her, whispered, "I think we've known each other long enough for you to call me Murdock."

His touch was like an electric charge while his warm breath teased the sensitive cord of her neck. She wanted to lean back against him and have his arms wrap around her. Get out of here, she ordered herself. Nearly dropping the box of candy on a nearby table, she said, "Enjoy!" then quickly hurried into the kitchen.

Laying the flowers on the counter, she scowled at her trembling hands. He made her feel like a teenager on her first date. "But I'm not," she reminded herself. And she wasn't going to let a suit and tie, a few flowers and a box of candy throw her so off balance that she let down her guard.

But as her gaze fell on a perfectly shaped pink rose, she found herself admitting that he did look impressive and it was flattering that he'd gone to the trouble to formally court her. Thoughts like that can lead to pain, she warned herself and shoved them from her mind.

Moving without haste, she found a vase then began slowly arranging the flowers, cutting each stem and carefully placing each blossom individually in the water. With any luck, she figured she could spend better than half an hour at this job.

"Obviously I should have opted for an already arranged bouquet." Murdock's voice sounded from behind her. Startled, Irene jumped, nearly knocking over the huge vase.

Reaching around her, Murdock steadied it.

Irene realized she'd been concentrating so hard on the flowers to avoid thinking about him, she hadn't heard him come in. Now he was standing so close he was the only thing she could think about.

"Hiding out in here isn't going to work," he warned her as he took a step to the side so that he was beside her rather than behind her. Hooking his finger under her chin, he tilted her face upward. "I'd never have thought you would behave cowardly. You're much too strong a woman for that."

The confession that she didn't feel strong around him almost escaped. "I'm merely trying to avoid an uncomfortable situation," she said instead. "I've already told you I have no intention of falling for you."

"Then, since your mind is so firmly made up, spending a little time in my company shouldn't be difficult. We'll be

well chaperoned and even if we weren't, I give you my word,
I'll behave like a perfect gentleman."

Another reason for his persistence suddenly occurred to
Irene. "Are you sure you aren't here simply because I'm a
challenge to your male ego?"

He smiled sheepishly. "You're a challenge, all right, but
not to my ego. I never thought I'd fall so fast or so hard for
any woman. But I have and I'm not giving up without a
fight."

Irene felt her toes wanting to curl with delight at the husky
determination in his voice. Her body threatened to sway toward him. Afraid he might read her thoughts in her eyes, she
dropped her gaze from his face and it fell on the sleeve of his
coat. The image of his injured arms filled her mind. The
thought that he could be taken from her as quickly as Jack
had, caused a chill to spread through her. "You'll lose," she
warned him stiffly, her cool shield once again in place.

"Anything worth having is worth fighting for," he returned. "I'll just watch while you finish arranging those
flowers. I do like the way you move."

Every muscle in her body tensed as she returned her attention to the flowers. She ordered herself to concentrate on
the fragrant blossoms but instead she was acutely aware of
Murdock's gaze. It was almost like a physical touch. Hurriedly she clipped the rest of the stems and shoved them into
the vase. "Done," she announced, striding back into the
living room.

"Must have been a lot of flowers," Sarah observed dryly.

"Quite a few," Irene replied nonchalantly, seating herself in a chair by the fire.

"The candy is great," Jeremy said, carrying the box to his
mother. "Sarah and I left the chocolate covered cherry for
you because it's your favorite."

Forcing a smile, Irene picked up a specially foil-wrapped piece of candy from among the assortment. "There's enough candy here to last till Christmas," she observed, attempting to make light conversation for Jeremy's and Sarah's benefit.

"I don't believe in doing anything halfway," Murdock replied, from the kitchen doorway.

Sarah nodded approvingly. "Halfway only gets you to the middle of the bridge."

Even in the middle of the bridge Murdock would be a threat, Irene thought, watching her son offering the candy to the man. The two of them looked so natural together, she felt shaken. Maybe she should marry him for Jeremy's sake, she reasoned. But as her gaze narrowed on Murdock, she knew she would be lying if she tried to make herself believe it was Jeremy she was thinking of. There was no doubt in her mind that if she lowered her barrier even a fraction of an inch, she would find herself falling hard for Murdock Parnell.

Unexpectedly Murdock moved away from the wall where he'd been leaning. "I don't want to overstay my welcome," he said.

Irene's guard suddenly faltered. She'd steeled herself for a long evening. His abrupt announcement of his intention to depart made her feel suddenly deserted. I should be relieved, she scolded herself.

"You're still welcome," Jeremy insisted. "We could play a game on the computer," he suggested, pleadingly.

Mussing the boy's hair playfully, Murdock smiled down at him reassuringly. "I'll see you tomorrow."

"It was real nice of you to stop by," Sarah said, rising. She crossed to the closet and took out his coat. "And we'll enjoy the candy and flowers." She glanced pointedly at Irene as she added this.

Reminded of her manners, Irene rose, too. "Yes, thank you," she said with formal politeness as Sarah handed Murdock his coat and he pulled it on.

Crossing the room in two long strides, he came to a halt only inches from her. "Think of me," he ordered gruffly, then placed a light kiss on the tip of her nose.

Thinking of him seemed to be occupying the majority of her time these days, she admitted silently as he winked comradely in Jeremy's direction, then smiled one last time at Sarah before leaving.

For a long moment Irene stood staring at the door through which Murdock had exited. The warmth of his lips lingered on the tip of her nose. Then out of the corner of her eye she saw Jeremy watching her expectantly. A prickling on the side of her neck caused her to look in Sarah's direction. Sarah, too, was studying her. "I need a drink of water," she said, abruptly escaping to the kitchen.

Mistake! her inner voice screamed as the fragrance of the flowers greeted her. Her gaze drawn to the blooms, Murdock's command that she think of him echoed in her ears and his image filled her mind. He wasn't playing fair, she wailed silently. She'd told him why she couldn't fall in love with him but he was trying to make her do just that anyway.

Driving home, Murdock smiled as he recalled the disconcerted expression on Irene's face when he left so quickly. He'd wanted to stay but he'd decided that the only way to crack that shield she kept around herself was to keep her off balance. And he was sure his ploy was working. "On the other hand, I could be fooling myself," he muttered. "She could be breathing a huge sigh of relief right now."

His jaw firmed. He hadn't expected winning her to be easy, he reminded himself.

* * *

Irene awoke exhausted the next morning with a frustration hangover. All night Murdock had haunted her dreams. "Think of me," she muttered, repeating his order from the night before. She scowled at her blurry-eyed image in the mirror. That seemed to be all she had done. "And it's got to stop," she commanded herself.

But as she entered the kitchen to start the coffee, she glanced toward the back door and realized she'd half expected him to be waiting there. Even more disconcerting was that instead of being relieved that he wasn't, she experienced a pang of disappointment. "I'm just tired," she muttered under her breath.

Next she became acutely aware of the fragrance of the flowers filling the room. She tried to concentrate on measuring the coffee, but the image of Murdock standing by the table watching her arrange the blossoms came back to taunt her. By the time she plugged in the percolator, her nerves were on a brittle edge. Grabbing the vase of blossoms, she carried it into the living room and set it on the coffee table.

On her return to the kitchen, she began gathering ingredients to make a coffee cake.

"I hope you've come to your senses and are making that to impress Murdock," Sarah said as she entered the kitchen. "I know it's old-fashioned but I still believe the way to a man's heart is through his stomach."

"I am not making this for Murdock," Irene returned curtly. "I like to bake when I'm tense. It relaxes me."

Sarah smiled. "I suppose in your case 'tense' is a good sign provided it's Murdock who is causing the tension." Her gaze narrowed on her niece. "It is him, isn't it?"

"I can't believe he's being so persistent," Irene fumed. "I've explained to him that I have no intention of ever falling in love again."

Sarah shook her head. "Opportunity knocks but once. Well, in this case, you've been lucky. He's knocked a few extra times and he's still knocking on your door. But Murdock's a proud man—he's not going to keep coming here forever just to be told to get lost."

Irene let out a groan of impatience. "How many times do I have to tell people I don't want a husband!"

"Maybe you'd be more convincing if you didn't look so rattled or like you hardly got any decent sleep last night," Sarah suggested.

"It's natural to have trouble sleeping once in a while. That doesn't mean I've got a man on my mind who won't go away and let me have some peace." Irene clamped her mouth shut. Those last words had come out too harshly. Seeing the "I knew it" look on Sarah's face, she knew she'd just confirmed her aunt's suspicions. Deciding that talking was only going to get her in deeper, she returned her full attention to measuring out the ingredients for the cake.

"I think I'll walk down to the main road and get the newspaper," Sarah said, her tone triumphant.

Irene drew a grateful breath as she once again had the kitchen to herself. And for the next few minutes she even managed to concentrate on her baking. She was crumbling the cinnamon topping on the batter just before sticking the cake into the oven when Jeremy entered the kitchen.

"You're making your coffee cake," he said happily, peering around her. "I know Mr. Parnell's going to really like that."

She started to again declare that she wasn't making the cake for Murdock Parnell but stopped herself. That would only bring a frown to her son's face. "I just hope you like it," she said instead, implying that he was the sole reason she was baking this morning.

He smiled warmly. "I always like it. You know that."
Again hope showed in his eyes. "And Mr. Parnell will, too."

"As long as *you* like my cooking, that's all that matters," she replied, determined to make him understand she had not made the cake for Murdock.

But Jeremy wasn't paying any attention, she realized, noticing her son looking toward the back door with an uncertain expression.

"Should I get a can of worms ready before he gets here?" he asked abruptly. His mouth formed a thoughtful pout. "Yesterday he didn't need any." He suddenly smiled up at his mother. "Maybe he won't be needing any this morning, either." His grin broadened. "Maybe he'll just come courting."

"Now that's a thought to brighten my morning," Irene muttered under her breath as she shoved the cake into the oven.

An hour later Jeremy stood staring at the back door once again. This time there was disappointment mingled with worry on his face. "Do you think maybe Mr. Parnell is sick?" he asked, breaking his silence.

"I'm sure he's fine," Irene replied. She felt twice as exhausted as she had when she'd first woken. All during breakfast she waited for Murdock's knock on the door. But like the second shoe that never fell but kept the listener on edge waiting for it to drop, he hadn't arrived. "It's time to leave for school," she said firmly a second time.

Nodding, Jeremy slowly pulled on his coat and then picked up his book bag. On the back porch he paused to look across the lake. "I can see the Brockmans' boat still at the dock," he announced. He glanced over his shoulder at his mother. "Maybe we should check on him."

"I'm sure he's just fine," she repeated. "And if we don't hurry, you're going to miss your bus."

"Murdock probably decided he wanted to eat breakfast in a warmer, more friendly environment," Sarah interjected just loud enough for Irene to hear her.

Ignoring the remark, Irene pulled on her coat and followed her son outside.

"Maybe you should stop by and see if he's okay," Jeremy suggested, as he and his mother walked down to the main road.

"I'm sure he's just sleeping in. He is on vacation." Irene tried to reason with her son.

"The lights were on in the Brockmans' living room," Jeremy countered. "I looked out my window when I first got up. It was still dark and I saw them."

"He probably just forgot to turn them off," Irene replied. Then seeing the concern growing on her son's face, she breathed a resigned sigh. "All right. When I get back to the house, I'll give him a call."

Jeremy smiled with relief.

Mentally Irene cringed. What excuse was she going to use when Murdock answered? While she waited with her son for his bus and then walked back up the road to her house, this question plagued her. She didn't want to encourage Murdock but her son's concern had begun to rub off on her. "And I am responsible for the Brockman house and that could be interpreted to mean the care and well-being of their guests as well," she argued.

Back in her kitchen, she glanced at the phone as she hung her coat on its peg. She still hadn't come up with an excuse to give Murdock an early-morning call. Even more, she really didn't want to talk to him.

A solution suddenly presented itself. She could go the Brockman house and check their propane tank to make certain it wasn't running low. While she was there, she should also make certain leaves weren't blocking any of the drains, she added. And as she went around the outside of the house, she could just take a quick look through the windows as she passed them. She was bound to see him. Then she'd know he was all right and she'd be keeping her promise to Jeremy. Satisfied with this course of action, she went in search of Sarah to tell her aunt she would be gone for a while.

Entering the living room, she came to an abrupt halt. Sarah was standing in front of the large mirror that hung on the wall near the front door. She'd unbraided her hair and was brushing it out. The heavy straight ebony strands with a sprinkling of gray hairs mingled in hung nearly to the middle of Sarah's back.

Noticing her niece, Sarah smiled self-consciously. "I used to wear my hair free when I was much younger." As she spoke she gently scooped the strands back, gathering them at her nape and binding them with a wide barrette.

The way she'd left the hair loosely draped on either side of her face made Sarah look several years younger, Irene thought. It also had a softening effect on Sarah's features. And for the first time she could remember, Irene read a vulnerableness in her aunt's expression.

"This print is much too bright," Sarah suddenly announced, frowning down at the scarlet print dress she was wearing. "I used to wear pastels. Pink and pale green looked especially good on me." Her frowned deepened. "And a nice pair of tan slacks would be much more comfortable."

"I suppose they would," Irene said, feeling she should say something.

"I guess it was wearing a uniform ninety-eight percent of the time that caused me to develop a taste for colorful outfits when I was off duty," Sarah continued thoughtfully. She shook her head at the image in the mirror. "But they're not really *me*."

First plain sugar cookies and now pastels, Irene mused, studying her aunt with concern. "Is something wrong?" she asked worriedly. "Would you like to talk? I'm a good listener."

Sarah smiled reassuringly. "No. Nothing is *wrong*. I'm just feeling a little restless and extremely bored with the current me."

Irene crossed the room and gave her aunt a hug. "I would never describe you as boring."

Sarah returned the hug, then releasing her niece, she took another look at herself in the mirror and her jaw firmed with decision. "I'm going shopping. Want to come along?"

"I have a couple of things I need to take care of around here and I need to finish that dress I'm making for Margaret Kolinski," Irene replied, feeling relieved she wouldn't have to tell Sarah she was going over to the Brockman house. She knew her aunt would never buy her excuses.

"Have fun," Sarah said. Then she cast a final approving grin at her new image in the mirror and with the excited sparkle in her eyes of a person setting out on an adventure, she went in search of her purse and coat.

A few minutes later, Irene stood on the porch waving goodbye to her aunt. Exploring new paths was all right for some people but she preferred to remain with the status quo, she reaffirmed.

As she walked to the Brockman house, she hoped she could complete her inspections without drawing Murdock's attention. Besides, maybe her aunt was right. Maybe, after last night, he'd decided to give up on her. This thought was supposed to cheer her up. Instead it brought a wave of depression. Angry with her duplicity, she picked up her pace. The sooner she finished this chore, the better.

Reaching the house, she made her way slowly around to the back, glancing in the windows on the lower level as she went. Jeremy was right. The lights were on. But she didn't see Murdock. Quickly she checked the pressure gage on the propane tank. It was a little better than sixty percent full. She'd known it would be. She'd checked it the first day Murdock had arrived.

She felt foolish being there. Still, the fact that she hadn't seen Murdock nagged her. Checking the drains, she made her way slowly around the entire house, glancing in the windows as she passed. She caught no glimpse of him. Standing, frowning at the back door, she knew she was going to have to go up there and knock. She couldn't leave without knowing for certain that he was not injured or ill.

"I never would have thought of you as a Peeping Tom."

Irene jerked around, to see Murdock behind her.

"Jeremy was concerned when you didn't come by this morning," she blurted. "I promised him I'd check on you." Not wanting him to think her sole reason for coming here was because of him, she added quickly, "Besides, I needed to check on the drains and the gas tank."

His gaze searched her face. "When I got back last night, Horace had called. He needed me to work out a software problem for him. I've been up all night."

He did look tired. Worry for him flooded through her. "You should get some sleep."

"I was just about to when I saw you coming up the road."

The intensity of his gaze was unnerving. She had to get out of there. "Well, I'm finished here now."

As she started to walk away, he stepped in front of her, blocking her path. "I could have sworn I saw genuine concern for me in your eyes just now."

"I feel responsible for any guest the Brockmans' have," she returned.

He frowned at her answer and the tiredness on his face increased. He started to step out of her way, then stopped. "Have dinner with me tonight, here, just the two of us."

The desire to accept his invitation was almost overwhelming. Danger signals flashed in her head. "I can't," she said with finality and, circling him, headed around to the front of the house.

But as she started down the road on her way home she experienced a sense of emptiness so intense her stomach knotted. Glancing over her shoulder, she saw him standing by the side of the house watching her. His expression was grim and she wanted desperately to gently caress his cheek and try to bring a smile to his face. She stopped and turned around to face him. "What time?" she yelled back at him.

"Six," came his reply.

She nodded, then quickly turned and walked on. Inside she felt like jelly. A part of her warned her that she should never have accepted the invitation while another part couldn't wait for the long day to pass.

Murdock stood stunned. His exhaustion had caused him to consider giving up. Only the concern in her eyes had given him the encouragement to ask her to dinner. Her refusal had made him wonder if perhaps he was kidding himself into thinking he could make her care enough about him to forget her fear. When she'd turned back and accepted his invitation, his heart had actually seemed to lurch. Now he felt like letting out a roar of triumph. "Well, one of us is acting like a school kid," he muttered under his breath. "And this *kid* had better get some rest so he doesn't make a complete fool of himself tonight."

"You look preoccupied," Sarah remarked as she and Irene sat eating lunch.

"And you look lovely," Irene replied honestly, not wanting to talk about what was on her mind. During her walk home from the Brockman place, a solution to her dilemma over Murdock had began to play through Irene's mind. At first she'd rejected it, but it had lingered. Finally she'd decided it could be the answer. However, she was afraid her aunt would be shocked. She, herself, was still feeling shaky and insecure about what she was considering doing. Sarah smiled crookedly.

"I do feel rather comfortable."

Irene smiled back at her aunt. Sarah was now clothed in a pair of tan corduroy slacks and a pale green sweater, the color of which gave a greenish tint to her gray eyes. Her aunt, Irene had noticed when Sarah had appeared in this outfit, had a very nice figure. It was trim with well-proportioned feminine curves. Sarah was also still wearing her hair in the casual, becoming style into which she'd arranged it before her shopping trip. All in all, her aunt looked very becoming, Irene reasserted mentally.

Sarah's smile disappeared as her gaze leveled on her niece. "You, however, do not appear to be the least bit comfortable. You look like a woman with something serious on her mind."

"I'm having dinner with Murdock tonight," Irene replied, knowing she was going to have to tell her aunt sooner or later. Suddenly feeling guilty about leaving Sarah to baby-sit Jeremy for a second time, she added, "That is, if you don't mind looking after Jeremy. But if you'd rather I stayed at home, I could cancel." She found herself half hoping her aunt might want her to remain home thus providing her with an excuse to escape the dinner with Murdock. However, considering Sarah's attempts at matchmaking she was sure this would not be the case.

Providing proof Irene had judged rightly, approval sparkled on Sarah's face. "Of course I want you to go. Jeremy and I will have a fine time here by ourselves."

Irene forced a grateful smile while wondering if her aunt would look so approving if Sarah knew what she was planning. Her stomach again tightened and the sandwich she was eating lost its appeal.

Sarah frowned. "You look as nervous as a turkey just before Thanksgiving."

Irene gave what she hoped was a nonchalant shrug. "It's been a long time since I shared an intimate dinner with a man."

"Too long," Sarah declared. She gave her niece an encouraging smile. "Relax. Enjoy yourself."

"I hope to," Irene replied. Again forcing a nonchalance into her voice, she added, "I need to run a couple of errands this afternoon so I'll stop by the school and pick up Jeremy on my way home." Then using the excuse that she wanted to get Margaret's dress finished before Monday, she rose and began clearing away the dishes.

Chapter Ten

It was late afternoon. Irene had run her errands and picked up Jeremy. Now she stood at her dresser placing her purchases from the drugstore into her purse. A tinge of embarrassment gave a pink tint to her cheeks.

She'd left early enough to drive to Pine River and use a drugstore there, which she'd only been in once before several years ago. She'd told herself that it was nobody's business but her own what she bought. However, she knew everyone who worked at Krindles Drugstore in Hares Burrow and her desire for privacy made it impossible for her to convince herself to buy condoms there.

But simply driving to Pine River had not proved to be as successful a ploy as she'd hoped. When she walked up to the cash register to pay for her purchases, Rosemary Robins had suddenly come out of the back to wait on her. Rosemary was not only a resident of Hares Burrow, but her youngest son was in the same grade as Jeremy, and Irene and Rosemary had worked together on several school projects. However, instead of the raised eyebrow Irene had expected to receive, Rosemary had merely given her nod of approval. "Always a smart idea to have some protection around," the woman had said and Irene's embarrassment had diminished a little.

Her nervousness, however, had continued to remain strong. Maybe her plans for the evening weren't such a good idea, she cautioned herself again. Well, she could always change her mind, she countered. But in case she didn't, at least she'd taken the proper precautions.

A knock on her bedroom door caused her to jump and quickly click the purse shut. The knock sounded again. "Come in," she responded calmly.

Jeremy entered the room and being careful not to slam the door, closed it behind him. Then keeping his voice low, he asked, "What's happened to Aunt Sarah?"

Irene couldn't help smiling at her son's perplexity. "She just decided she wanted to change her appearance a little."

Jeremy frowned thoughtfully. "I liked her the way she was." After a moment, he added, "But she does look nice this way, too."

"Everyone needs a change in their life once in a while," Irene said, and realized she was talking as much about herself as she was about Sarah.

Jeremy suddenly smiled. "Going out with Mr. Parnell will be a nice change for you."

Irene recalled how excited he'd been during the ride home from school after she'd told him about her date with Murdock. "It's only a date," she reminded him.

"I know," he replied, then smiling so broadly his whole face seemed like a grin, he left.

As the door closed behind him, Irene took a deep breath. It was only a date but it could also be an adventure into very new territory for her. Her nervousness multiplied.

* * *

"Relax, go with the flow. Take your time. You've got all evening to decide if you really want to go through with your plan," she told herself for the umpteenth time as she approached the Brockman house. She'd chosen to walk, hoping the exercise and the cool night breeze would help calm her jittery nerves. But as she neared the porch, the urge to flee was strong.

Then the door opened and Murdock's muscular bulk filled the doorway. Desire stirred within her. No longer able to fight her attraction for him, she mounted the steps.

"I thought you might have changed your mind," he said, stepping aside to allow her to enter.

Glancing at the clock, she saw she was fifteen minutes late. Not wanting to admit she'd changed clothes three times and was about to change back into her first choice when Jeremy and Sarah had both blocked the door of her bedroom and insisted she looked wonderful, she smiled demurely and lied. "Sarah wanted to send along a dessert and I had to wait a couple of minutes for it to come out of the oven."

The brown of his eyes darkened with pleasure. "I'm sure both it and you will be worth the wait."

She handed him the pie plate and while he carried it to the kitchen, she slipped her coat off. Hanging it on a peg near the door, she made a quick inspection of herself in the mirror. The dress she was wearing was the one she'd originally wanted to choose but it had taken until her third attempt to work up her courage to put it on. It was a clinging black knee-length jersey that fit her contours like a glove. The neckline was high, culminating in a turtleneck but the shoulders were cut away.

She'd bought it because it made her feel sexy but she'd never worn it in public. Jack had refused to allow her out of the house in it. Her thick black hair was hanging loose and free down her back. At the drugstore, she'd found a pair of sheer black panty hose with a single line of design down the side of each leg. Her shoes, black leather wedgies, had been a concession to walking down a gravel road. However, taking in the full effect, she was pleased with all her choices. High heels would have been too formal for the effect she wanted to create.

Giving herself a mental nod of approval, she strode toward the seating grouping by the fireplace. A low whistle brought her to a halt. Glancing in the direction from which it had come, she saw Murdock in the door of the living room. His gaze played over her and a very masculine glint showed in his eyes.

"You do know how to put a strain on a man's control," he said.

She smiled nervously. The dress was having the desired effect.

"Would you like some wine?" he offered.

Wine could help relax her, she reasoned. "Yes, thank you," she replied, fighting to keep the stiff edge out of her voice.

His gaze again traveled over her. "I think I'll skip it," he mumbled as he pulled his attention away and poured her a glass.

She found herself liking the fact that he seemed so disconcerted. A sense of womanly power flowed through her. Then he handed her the glass and his fingers brushed against hers. The heat of his touch raced through her, igniting a fire that threatened to consume her. The power she had over him seemed suddenly infinitesimal.

The effect he's having on me is merely a physical thing and tonight will be the beginning of the cure, she assured herself, smiling seductively up at him.

Confusion showed on Murdock's face, then his expression suddenly lightened. "Can I assume you've decided to stop fighting me and are ready to set the date for our wedding?" he asked huskily.

"Not exactly." She took a sip of the wine to bolster her courage.

He studied her questioningly. "What do you mean by 'not exactly'?"

"I mean I've decided to stop fighting the attraction I feel for you," she replied.

He grinned triumphantly. "I'm glad to hear that." Obviously forcing himself to move cautiously, he did not embrace her but merely leaned forward and kissed her lightly on the lips. "With that attitude it should only be a matter of time before I convince you to set the date," he said as he straightened away from her.

Irene's gaze hardened. "I'm not going to marry you or anyone."

Again Murdock looked confused. "Maybe you'd better explain what's going on in that pretty little head of yours because I sure can't figure it out."

Irene swallowed the lump of nervousness that had suddenly formed in her throat. She'd meant to ease into this subject but it was too late now for finesse. Besides, she was too tense to be coy. "I was thinking we could have an affair."

Surprise replaced his confusion. "An affair?"

"According to the magazines and television talk shows, people are doing it all the time," she replied, working hard to keep a nonchalance in her voice.

His gaze narrowed. "You actually came here tonight intending to end up in my bed?"

"I came prepared for that possibility," she admitted, fighting a threatened bout of giddiness.

He raised an eyebrow quizzically. "Prepared?"

"Protection," she elaborated. "I'm not stupid or careless."

"I suppose I should be relieved to hear that," he muttered.

Irene felt the glow of embarrassment spreading from her neck upward. She'd expected a more enthusiastic response from him. Then she saw the cold cynicism beginning to form in his eyes and her embarrassment multiplied. She had to get out of there. Retreat with dignity, she ordered herself. "If you're not interested, I think I should leave," she said, setting her glass down on the coffee table.

The cynicism turned to the unmasked anger of a man who felt he'd been duped. "Is this the way you fight your loneliness? With affairs? Short flings? One-night stands?" he growled.

Pride refused to allow him to think she would behave so wantonly. "No. This is the first time I've ever considered anything like this," she returned with self-righteous defensiveness.

Confusion mingled with the anger on his face. "You'll have an affair with me but you won't consider marrying me."

Irene's back stiffened. "That's right." Her embarrassment was now more than she could stand. "Obviously this has been more of a shock to you than I thought it would be. I'll just leave and let you think about it."

As she tried to circle the couch, he blocked her way. "Why?" he demanded curtly. "Why an affair but never marriage? Are you still worried about losing your independence?"

"I'm worried about losing my heart." Irene gasped as this confession echoed in her ears. Resolve etched itself into her features. "I want to be with you but I will not fall in love with you."

"You want a strictly physical relationship," he said, clarifying her intentions.

"Strictly physical," she confirmed.

For a long moment he studied her. Suddenly total comprehension flashed in his eyes and a grimness descended over his features. "You want a relationship with no emotional commitment so you won't feel any loss if it should come to an end."

His scrutiny was unnerving her. "Yes," she admitted tersely.

His gaze turned to ice. "Well, thanks but no thanks. I'm not looking for a part-time playmate. I want a woman who's not afraid to care." He backed away from her, then abruptly turned and stalked out of the room.

Irene stood like a statue staring at the now empty space Murdock had so recently occupied. A painful sense of having been abandoned swept through her. It's only my pride being injured, she told herself. Forcing her legs to move, she retrieved her coat and purse and left.

Murdock had come to an abrupt halt in the hall just beyond the living-room door. He stood there silently cursing. He wasn't certain who he was most angry with . . . Irene for being so stubbornly insular or the inborn instinct that ruled his heart for choosing her out of all the other women in the world. The coldness in his eyes intensified. "Good riddance," he declared under his breath, hearing the front door open and close.

Walking back into the living room, he caught a light whiff of her perfume. The desire to hold her was close to overwhelming. The thought that maybe he should have taken her up on her offer, that maybe that would have gotten her out of his system, played through his mind. "Or, more likely, I would have just been asking for more trouble," he muttered. His jaw steeled into a line of resolve. Clearly his inherited instinct for finding a mate had seriously erred. Irene Galvin was one lady he would be smart to forget he ever met.

His gaze shifted to the window. Clouds covered the moon and stars, producing a murky blackness. The scowl on his face darkened. "She doesn't want or need my protection," he grumbled at himself. But even so, he found himself grabbing his coat and pulling it on as he stormed out of the house.

Irene heard the slamming of the door and the crunch of gravel behind her. The thought that Murdock had changed his mind brought a rush of hope. She stopped and turned to see him coming toward her. Happiness filled her. The urge to run into his arms was so powerful it frightened her. She simply missed the physical intimacy of being with a man...that was all that was causing the joy she was experiencing, she assured herself. Ordering herself to move with dignity, she took a step toward him.

Murdock held up his hand like a traffic cop stopping an oncoming car. "I'm here to make sure you get home safely. After that you're on your own," he growled.

Hot tears of disappointment burned at the back of her eyes. "I can get home by myself," she replied stiffly.

"Don't argue with me," he snapped. "Don't say anything. Just walk."

The intensity of his anger convinced her there could never be anything but animosity between them. Any attraction he'd felt for her had been destroyed. Now my life can get back to the way it was, she told herself. But this thought didn't bring the sense of peace she'd hoped for. Instead she continued to remain tense and uneasy.

She found herself wanting to say something to him, wanting to lessen his ire toward her. She glanced at him.

As if he'd guessed what was on her mind, he warned sharply, "Don't say anything unless you've decided to let that barrier you're keeping around your heart crumble."

"I never want to feel that vulnerable again," she returned through clenched teeth, the words as much for herself as for him.

Silence again filled the air between them. When they reached her front porch, he stopped at the foot of the steps. Alone, she continued onto the porch. But as she reached the door and her hand closed around the knob, politeness insisted she thank him for seeing her home. She turned back to him, but before she could utter a word, he abruptly turned away from her and started down the road in long, purposeful strides.

Watching him, she knew that was the end of Murdock Parnell in her life.

"That was a fast dinner," Sarah remarked as Irene entered the house and closed the door. "Jeremy and I sat down to the table as soon as you left and I just finished clearing up a moment ago."

"Murdock and I have decided that we are not right for each other, after all," she announced, bracing herself for an argument from both her aunt and her son.

But Sarah didn't offer any protest. Instead she said with acceptance, "I am sorry to hear that. I like him. But if the chemistry isn't there, it simply isn't there."

Jeremy, who had been doing his homework seated on the floor in front of the fireplace, rose and approached Irene. There was a shadow of regret in his eyes but there was understanding on his face. "Aunt Sarah and I had a long talk during dinner. She explained to me that sometimes two very nice people just don't get along with each other. I guess that's you and Mr. Parnell.'' As a show of support, he slipped his hand into his mother's. ''I'll miss him, but we did just fine before he came and we'll do just fine when he leaves.''

Irene knelt and hugged her son tightly. ''Yes, we will,'' she said with assurance. Then after casting Sarah a ''thank you'' glance, she went into her room and changed.

A few minutes later she was foraging in the kitchen for food. She'd been too nervous to eat anything since breakfast. Now, suddenly she was ravenous. As she carved off a piece of baked chicken, Sarah entered.

''I really appreciate you talking to Jeremy,'' she said before shoving the bite into her mouth and cutting off another.

''I don't like to see either of you unhappy. I'm glad I could help,'' Sarah replied.

Irene ate another bite while her aunt poured herself a cup of coffee. Murdock's image suddenly filled Irene's mind and the food threatened to stick in her throat. She forced the bite down and his image out. But her hunger had vanished. She put the chicken away.

''Do you want to talk?'' Sarah asked gently.

''There's nothing to talk about,'' Irene replied, seating herself at the table and resting her chin in her hands. ''He wants a commitment and I can't give him one.'' Regret etched itself into her features. ''I know I may be making the biggest mistake of my life, but I can't face letting myself love him and then possibly lose him.''

''We all have our private demons,'' Sarah said soothingly. She laid her hand on Irene's shoulder. ''Some are worse than others but keep in mind...a coward dies a thousand small deaths.''

''He who runs may live to fight another day.'' Irene tossed back.

"But the battle lost may have been the decisive one. A bridge burned cannot ever be rebuilt exactly as it was," Sarah said in rebuttal.

Catching the sudden uneasy note in her aunt's voice, Irene looked up at her. There was a faraway look in Sarah's eyes and Irene had the distinct impression her aunt wasn't thinking about her. "Are we talking about bridges I'm burning or ones you've burned?" she asked.

"Ward Anders and I were on the verge of becoming engaged when we fought and broke up," Sarah said slowly, more as if she was talking to herself than to Irene. "I didn't try to patch things up. I left. At the time it seemed like the right thing to do. But sometimes I wonder."

Glad to be talking about someone other than herself, Irene asked, "Do you know whatever happened to him?"

"He married and had a couple of children. I heard he was widowed a couple of years ago."

Irene studied her aunt with interest. "Have you ever considered going to see him to see if the old spark is still there?"

"A spark once fully smoldered cannot ever be rekindled," Sarah replied. "Besides, I don't believe in living in the past or dwelling on the 'what might have beens.' I believe in people getting on with their lives."

Mentally Irene groaned. Certain she was in for another bout of advice from her aunt, she braced herself.

Unexpectedly Sarah opened a cabinet and began taking out plates. "But enough about the men in our lives. A piece of cake and a glass of milk. That's what we need. They're always soothing to the soul after a difficult day," she said.

Both startled and relieved by her aunt's sudden decision to turn the conversation to food, Irene watched in silence as Sarah poured two glasses of milk, set them on the table, then cut two huge pieces from the cake she'd baked that afternoon.

Still, as hard as she tried to keep him at bay, Murdock threatened to reenter Irene's mind. She pushed him out and concentrated on the cake. "What's the special ingredient?" she asked as Sarah set one of the plates in front of her and seated herself across the table with the other.

"It's just plain white cake with chocolate icing," Sarah replied. Looking down at her piece, she frowned. "I don't know why I made it. My grandmother used to make it for Sam Raven. He worked for my grandparents. He was only a couple of years older than me but he always treated me as if I were a mere child compared to him or, at the least, that I was mildly addleheaded."

Irene studied her aunt thoughtfully. Sarah was scowling down at her piece of cake. "He seems to have made quite an impression on you."

"He was a mixture of Cheyenne and Shoshoni. His Indian name was Rumbling Thunder and it fit him well." Sarah gave a sharp shrug of her shoulder. "I don't know why I even thought of him. I suppose everyone has at least one irritating nuisance in their life they can never quite erase from their memory."

Murdock's image again filled Irene's mind. "I suppose," she replied solicitously as she forced the image out once again.

Sarah forked a piece of the cake. But with it barely halfway to her mouth, she stopped. Defiance sparked in her eyes. She returned the fork still holding the uneaten bite of cake to her plate then shoved her chair away from the table. "I don't need these calories. What I need is a brisk walk," she announced.

Irene had never seen Sarah rattled. "I'll come with you," she offered, concerned about her aunt.

Sarah had carried her plate of cake to the sink. Setting it down, she turned to her niece. "Normally I'd enjoy your company, but I've got some thinking to do.'' Before Irene could say any more, Sarah grabbed her coat from a peg by the door and left.

"It would seem that Aunt Sarah has a ghost or two in her past she hasn't been able to exorcise,'' Irene noted, forking herself a piece of the cake.

Murdock's face returned to fill her inner vision. Memories of him weren't going to remain to torment her, she assured herself. After all, she'd barely known him a week and he'd be gone soon. After that, she'd forget he ever existed. Probably within a few days, she'd even forget exactly what he looked like.

Chapter Eleven

Irene lay staring up at the ceiling. It was Saturday. Outside the sun was already up. Last night, after she'd eaten her cake, she played a couple of games with Jeremy, then watched some television with Sarah after he'd gone to bed. But she'd still been tense when she'd come up to her room and it had taken her a while to fall asleep.

Now, even though she'd slept past her usual waking time, she still felt tired. She considered continuing to lie there, snuggled under her blanket in her private sanctuary. At least here she didn't have to worry about running into Murdock.

She frowned at herself. Hiding out up here was not only cowardly, but it was impossible. She'd already heard the sound of pans in the kitchen. Sarah was up and probably Jeremy as well. She couldn't neglect them. Forcing herself out of bed, she got dressed and went downstairs.

"Aunt Sarah's making old-fashioned buckwheat pancakes," Jeremy announced as Irene joined them in the kitchen. "And I was wondering if I could ask Billy to come over and play today."

Irene knew her son well. The enthusiasm he usually exhibited when asking to have his friend over for the day was missing. She was sure his original plan had been to tag around after Murdock today if the man would allow him. But because of her, he was now seeking another entertainment. Playing with Billy would be better for him anyway, she reasoned. Murdock would be leaving never to return. Jeremy would only be hurt if his attachment to the man grew stronger. "Having Billy over sounds like a terrific idea," she replied.

"I'll call him after breakfast," Jeremy said, some of the enthusiasm she was used to hearing entering his voice.

Jeremy was going to survive Murdock's leaving just fine, Irene assured herself. And she'd be glad when the man was gone, she added, refusing to acknowledge the nudge of regret deep within.

Murdock stood at the window gazing out over the lake. The lights had been on at the Galvin house for a while now and in his mind's eye he could picture Sarah, Irene and Jeremy gathered around the breakfast table.

He scowled at himself. He'd come here to relax. Instead he'd found Irene Galvin. Her offer to have an affair had taunted him all night. He'd woken restless and tense. "It's time I got out of here before I do something I'll regret," he growled under his breath.

Sarah had just placed a plate of pancakes in front of Irene when a knock sounded on the back door.

"It's Mr. Parnell," Jeremy said, seeing the man through the window. He was out of his chair in a flash. But halfway to the door, he suddenly stopped abruptly in midstride and

urned back to his mother. Uncertainty had replaced the
welcoming smile on his face.

"Go let him in," Sarah ordered, with a shooing motion
of her hand.

"Of course, you should let him in," Irene echoed when
her son did not move but continued to watch her worriedly
as if afraid she didn't want Murdock in their house. "Mr.
Parnell and I are not enemies," she added, not wanting him
to feel as if he had to take sides between her and the man.

Jeremy's expression relaxed and he resumed his dash to
the door.

"Would you like some pancakes?" Sarah offered, already pouring batter into the skillet as Murdock entered.

"No, thanks," he replied, stopping just inside the door.
"I've decided the time has come for me to go home."

A sudden sadness swept through Irene. This is what you
wanted, she chided herself. "Have a safe trip," she said and
marveled at how calm and unemotional she'd sounded. Inside, she wanted to cry. Then she looked up at him and saw
the frost in his eyes. Whether he went or stayed would make
no difference now, she knew. She'd managed to kill any fire
he'd felt for her.

Murdock's gaze shifted to Sarah. "Thanks for the food.
It opened whole new taste experiences for me."

Irene noticed that a warmth entered his eyes when he addressed her aunt and envy swept through her. You got what
you wanted, her inner voice reminded her.

The warmth in Murdock's gaze deepened as he turned to
Jeremy. "It's been a real pleasure knowing you," he said,
extending his hand to the boy.

Accepting the man's handshake, Jeremy flushed with
pleasure. "It's been a real pleasure knowing you, too."

"Will you walk me to my car?" Murdock requested. "I
left something out there I'd like you to have."

Jeremy glanced over his shoulder at his mother. Clearly he didn't entirely believe her claim that she and Murdock were not at war. She gave him a nod of approval and he preceded the man out the door.

The urge to go to the window for one last look at Murdock was too strong for Irene to resist. She saw him giving Jeremy a rod and reel. Her son's face was filled with excitement. Murdock was grinning crookedly, a sort of boyish grin that let her know he was pleased with Jeremy's reaction.

Unexpectedly Murdock glanced toward the house. His expression became cool and she knew he'd seen her. Embarrassed to have been caught watching him, she took a step back. He scowled impatiently, then returned his attention to her son. A solemnness came over the two male faces as he extended his hand to Jeremy. Her son looked suddenly very adult as he accepted the handshake, Irene thought. She saw Murdock nod with satisfaction, then climb into his car and leave. And that's the end of that, she told herself.

Turning back to the table, she noticed Sarah watching her. "You look like a woman who might be feeling some regret," her aunt observed.

"I'm not," she replied firmly, but deep inside there was a hard knot of pain. By tomorrow it will be gone, she assured herself. Even more to the point, Murdock was gone and from the chill in his eyes, she knew he never wanted to see her again. "What's done is done," she added.

At that moment Jeremy came in. "Mr. Parnell gave me this great rod and reel." He held up his gift for his aunt and mother to see.

"Very nice," Sarah replied approvingly.

Jeremy gave her a quick quirky smile then turned to his mother. Again she saw the worry on his face as if he wasn't certain she would be as approving as Sarah. "I told him he

lidn't have to give me anything," he said, a defensive edge
n his voice.

She forced a soft smile to reassure him that the gift was all
ight with her. "That was very thoughtful of him. Looks
ike a very nice rod and reel."

His expression relaxed. "It is." His gaze turned to the
ishing equipment he was holding. A shadow of sadness
lickered over his features. "I'll put it away before I call
3illy."

Irene saw the flicker of sadness and knew her son was
ighting to hide his regret that Murdock was gone. A re-
sponding sadness swept through her. Suddenly the walls of
the house felt as if they were closing in on her. "Wait," she
blurted as Jeremy headed for the door.

He turned, the worry back on his face.

"I was just thinking that we three could go into town today, have lunch and see a movie," she suggested.

The worry on Jeremy's face was replaced by a relieved
grin. "Sure, if that's what you want to do," he agreed, then
asked, "Can I have popcorn?"

"You can have all the popcorn you can eat," she promised.

Sarah closed the cookbook she'd been perusing. "Sounds
like fun to me."

"Then let's get these breakfast dishes washed and get going," Irene ordered.

"Have you finally run out of steam?" Sarah asked.

Irene looked up to see her aunt coming out of the kitchen
to join her on the back porch. It was Sunday afternoon and
for the past few minutes Irene had been sitting in a rocking
chair watching Jeremy and Billy fishing down on the dock.

"Yesterday you kept us busy with shopping, a movie,
then games after dinner," Sarah continued, seating herself

on the porch rail so she could face Irene. "This morning
was church. Then you invited Jeremy's little friend to joi
us for dinner and stay the afternoon. While he and Jerem
have been playing, you've raked the leaves, gotten you
gardens cleared of dead plants and chopped enough kir
dling to start fires for the next month."

"There's always a lot to do around here," Irene replie
defensively, refusing to admit she'd been keeping busy so sh
wouldn't think about Murdock.

"When Jack died, you cleaned this house from cellar t
attic. I remember that because your mother was worrie
you'd make yourself sick working too hard. But she knev
it was your way of keeping your mind occupied so's not t
dwell on your loss. So, she kept you fed and made certai
you got some sleep."

Irene frowned up at her aunt. "This isn't the same thin;
at all. I'm merely getting a few chores out of the way so yo
and I can spend more time together next week. I feel as i
I've been neglecting you."

"You haven't," Sarah assured her. "This visit has bee
good for me. I've had time to do some thinking I needed t
do." She frowned thoughtfully. "Maybe it's a family trait."

Irene regarded her aunt questioningly. "What's a famil
trait?"

"Keeping busy so we don't face our real feelings," Sarah
elaborated. "In your case, you clean, rake, chop wood. Me,
I joined the navy and since I've gotten out, I've busied my
self taking temporary but interesting jobs, doing favors fo
old friends, visiting family members along with worrying
about their problems and trying to help when I can." With
out waiting for a response, she turned and went back in
side.

Irene drew a shaky breath. This wasn't anything like when
Jack had died, she assured herself. In no time at all, she'd

forget about Murdock and have her life back on an even keel. Noticing that a few more leaves had fallen, she eased herself out of the chair and found her rake.

Irene's hand closed around the knob of the Brockmans' front door. It was now Monday morning. Jeremy was back in school, Sarah was writing letters and the time had come for Irene to clean the Brockmans' house.

Ever since Murdock had left, she'd been wanting to get this job over with. Cleaning the house of any remaining signs he'd ever been here would, she was sure, allow her to put him out of her mind once and for all. But during the school year, she made herself save her weekends for family time. Thus, she'd forced herself to wait until today to tackle this cathartic cleansing.

She frowned at her hesitation to enter and thrust the door open. Memories of encounters with Murdock assailed her. Hot tears burned at the back of her eyes. "Clean!" she ordered herself.

But as she stripped his bed, she found herself imagining him there. She could almost see him as he had been a week ago, caught in the throngs of a nightmare. Suddenly she found herself wishing she could be with him to help when he had another. "I'm sure he can find plenty of women to volunteer to come to his aid," she told herself. This thought didn't bring the relief she'd hoped. Instead it caused a sharp jab of pain.

"Get out of here," she ordered herself and grabbing up the sheets hurried to the laundry room.

After getting the washing machine started, she headed into the kitchen. This room did not arouse any intense memories. As she wiped the counters, waxed the furniture, then mopped the floor, she was able to focus her full concentration on her job. Breathing a sigh of relief, she assured herself that her cleaning of this house was having the cathartic effect she'd hoped.

But as she entered the living room, her Friday night encounter with Murdock began playing through her mind. The masculine approval she'd read in his face when he'd first seen her dress brought a crooked smile to her lips. But it quickly disappeared as she recalled the anger in his eyes when he realized she wanted nothing more than a physical relationship. A knot of regret so tight it hurt formed in her abdomen. Her chin trembled.

"He's gone. Forget him," she ordered herself. Forcing her mind to her task, she cleaned the room. "Done," she announced as she wiped the last speck of dust from the mantel.

A fresh wave of tension curled up her back. She could no longer avoid the upstairs. "There's nothing left of him here," she assured herself, as she climbed the stairs.

Wrong! she groaned unhappily as she entered the bathroom. Even though it was very, very faint, she caught the lingering scent of his after-shave and a yearning so intense that her legs threatened to weaken swept through her. "So I fell in love with him," she admitted grimly, unable to deny the truth any longer.

As she finished cleaning the house, his presence seemed to surround her. He'd come into her life barely over a week ago and yet she was missing him as much as if he'd been a part of her world for months...years, she confessed tiredly as she put her supplies away. "But I'll get over him," she stated, assuring herself that her memories would be less intense when she left this house.

But outside, his presence continued to haunt her. Walking home, she recalled her trips down this gravel road with him. Everything seemed to remind her of him, she wailed silently. Deep within she felt a void as if a vital part of her life was missing. Back in her own home, even Sarah's company didn't lessen or even slow down the growing loneliness pervading her.

Impatiently she waited for Jeremy's return from school, hoping his presence would help. As he climbed off the bus, just having him with her did cheer her up some. Still the void remained.

As she, Sarah and Jeremy sat eating dinner, Irene tried hard to concentrate on what her son was saying. He was explaining about a new game he'd learned in gym class but his words were being blurred by a growing sense of anxiety that threatened to permeate every cell of her body. The agonizing sensation that she was allowing something very precious to slip away tormented her. Suddenly the thought that had been nagging at her all day, burst forth. "I need to go see Murdock," she blurted, then grimaced self-consciously as her words were met with stunned looks from her son and her aunt.

Jeremy's surprise quickly turned to confusion. "I thought you didn't like him. I thought you were glad he was gone."

"I wasn't being honest with him or myself," she replied, tired of hiding the emotions brewing within her. "I do like him. I like him a lot."

Sarah smiled with satisfaction. "I'm glad to hear you admitting that at last."

Recalling the ice she'd seen in Murdock's eyes the last time he looked her way, Irene's anxiousness grew. "But I may be too late."

"I'm sure you can patch things up with him," Jeremy said encouragingly.

"I will try," Irene promised.

"I suggest you pack a bag and get going. A minute wasted is a minute lost," Sarah coaxed.

A plea spread over Irene's face as she turned to her aunt. "Would you mind taking care of Jeremy for a few days? This isn't going to be easy and I'd rather do it on my own."

"Of course, I'll be happy to stay with Jeremy," Sarah reassured her.

Irene returned her attention to her son. "You understand that I have to go alone, don't you?"

He nodded. "Aunt Sarah and I will have a nice visit," he said in an adult manner.

Irene drew a relieved breath and gave him a tight hug. Then straightening, she said, "I'll need to call the Brockmans to find out where to find Murdock." She looked Jeremy in the eye. "I know I've told you never to lie and I'm not going to lie to them. Not really. However, I don't want to go into any detail about why I'm looking for Murdock so I'm simply going to tell them that he left something behind I'd like to return to him."

Again the memory of his cold parting gaze came back to haunt her. He hadn't let her glares of "keep away" stop him, she reminded herself. Now it was her turn to brave the possibility of rejection.

"You don't need to call the Brockmans." Jeremy was pushing his chair away from the table as he spoke, a superior grin on his face. "He left me his business card with his home address and phone number on the back. He told me I should call if I ever needed help of any kind," he explained over his shoulder as he hurried out of the kitchen.

"Murdock's leaving his address with Jeremy is an encouraging sign," Irene said more to herself than to her aunt. "He, at least, left with a soft spot in his heart for one of us."

Sarah's gaze narrowed on her. "I hope you aren't getting cold feet."

Irene's jaw tightened with resolve. "No. I'll never have any peace if I don't go see him."

"Here it is," Jeremy proclaimed, bursting back into the room, clutching a small white card.

For a moment, as she read the card, Irene's courage faltered. Murdock wasn't just another employee. He was a vice president in Horace's company. It was likely he got back to Minneapolis and realized she would never have fit into his life. But she'd never know if she didn't go, she prodded herself. Besides, if he did reject her, that could be the cure she needed. Then, finally, she could get back to her life as it was before he'd entered it.

"If I leave within the hour I can be there before midnight," she said, rising from the table and moving to the door.

"I'm all for striking while the iron is hot but maybe it would be better if you got a good night's sleep before making the drive," Sarah suggested with motherly concern.

"I've got to go now," Irene tossed back over her shoulder.

Irene glanced at her watch. She'd made good time until she'd gotten lost trying to find Murdock's home. Now it was the stroke of midnight. The address on the back of the card was that of a sprawling ranch house in a quiet suburb on the outskirts of town. She recognized his car in the driveway. The curtains were drawn but there were lights on in the house.

Nervousness swept through her. Maybe she should wait until morning. What if he had a female friend in for the evening or even for the night? "Then I'll have my answer," she murmured under her breath and forced herself out of her car.

Reaching the front door, she pressed the doorbell. A ringing inside let her know it worked. She heard footsteps, then the door was opened and Murdock was standing in front of her. He looked tired. He was wearing slacks with a button-down shirt. The sleeves of the shirt were rolled up part way to his elbows. His hair was mussed as if he'd been combing it back with his fingers. "I'm sorry to bother you so late," she heard herself saying.

For a long moment he studied her in an icy silence, then stepping to one side said, "You'd better come in. It's cold out there."

There was no welcome in his voice and her courage faltered. He'd pursued her when she'd pushed him away, she reminded herself again. And he was worth fighting for. Just seeing him caused the void within her to diminish. Steeling herself, she stepped inside.

As he closed the door, she caught a glimpse of herself in the hall mirror. She should have taken time to put on some makeup, she scolded herself. Her face was pale and there were dark circles under her eyes. Then there was her clothes. She'd been in such a rush to get here, she hadn't even thought about changing into something more feminine. Instead, beneath her heavy denim jacket, she was wearing a pair of worn jeans and an old flannel shirt. "I hope I didn't interrupt your evening," she said stiffly, glancing toward the living room and again wondering if he had a date in there. If so, her embarrassment would be complete.

"I was just catching up on some work," he replied coolly. A sudden concern showed in his eyes. "Is Jeremy all right? Has something happened to him?"

"He's fine," she assured him, wishing that concern had been for her. But now it was gone and his gaze was frosty once again. "He misses you," she added.

Murdock's expression darkened as if a thought he didn't like had just occurred to him. "It that why you're here?" Cynicism etched itself into his features. "You've reconsidred my proposal and decided you could marry me for your son's sake? If so, I'm not willing to settle for that."

"I'm not here because of Jeremy." She met his gaze levelly. "I'm here because I haven't been able to stop thinking about you. I thought I could. But I can't."

Irene had hoped her confession would bring a warmth to his eyes. Instead he continued to study her silently. She felt nauseous. She'd made a complete fool of herself. Obviously his feelings for her hadn't run as deeply as he'd claimed. Most likely, he'd suddenly realized she'd merely been a challenge. Now he was searching for a way to politely tell her to get lost. Well, she'd save him the trouble. "Obviously I've made a mistake coming here."

As she took a step toward the door, his hand closed around her arm. "I need to know exactly what you mean when you say you can't stop thinking about me. During my drive home and ever since I got back, I've fought the desire to take you up on your offer of an affair. But I won't settle for a mere physical relationship. Not with you." His gaze burned into her. "Are you prepared to drop your guard and allow yourself to learn to care for me?"

"I do care for you," she confessed. Reaching up she touched his jaw. "I've fallen in love with you. I never thought I'd feel this way again."

The ice in his eyes melted. "When I left, I wanted to forget you. But instead, during the past three days, I've spent endless hours trying to think of ways to win you." He grinned crookedly. "I even called my father to ask for advice."

The heat of his gaze warmed her. "I hope this means your offer of marriage is still open," she said, going up on tiptoes and kissing him lightly.

"Like I told you, lady," he said gruffly. "If you want to share my bed, you're going to have to be willing to marry me."

"Just name the day," she murmured against his lips.

"As soon as we can get a license," he replied, his arms circling her and drawing her hard against him. "I've practiced a great deal of restraint during the past few days. But I'm only human."

"You've been more than admirable," she agreed. Her mouth formed a mock pout. "In fact, you've been frustratingly admirable."

"I plan to make up for that," he promised huskily as his mouth claimed hers.

"Considering the fact that we only had five days to make the arrangements, it was a wonderful wedding," Sarah said, giving Irene a hug, then collapsing into a nearby chair.

Irene had to agree as she, too, plopped into the companion chair. The ceremony had taken place in Murdock's home with Jeremy, Murdock's parents, Jack's parents, the Brockmans and Aunt Sarah in attendance. Inclement weather had prevented Irene's parents from flying down from Alaska but they'd sent their congratulations and promised to come visit as soon as possible. Following the ceremony, there had been a catered dinner. Now all the guests but Aunt Sarah had left.

"The food was great," Jeremy said.

Irene smiled at her son. He and Murdock were seated on the couch with their feet propped up on the coffee table looking tired, happy and stuffed.

"Are you two sure you don't want me to stay an extra day or two to take care of Jeremy while you get away by yourselves for a short honeymoon?" Sarah offered.

Murdock ruffled Jeremy's hair. "I think we need to spend ome time with our son."

Irene smiled softly as she recalled the conversation she nd Murdock had had when Sarah had first volunteered to emain and watch over Jeremy so they could have a honey-noon.

"As much as I'd like to have some time alone with you," he'd said to him, "I'm worried about Jeremy. He seems to e accepting all the changes in his life well but there are a lot. He's in a new town and he'll be starting a new school."

"He needs us here as a family." Murdock had continued her thought when she paused, letting her know he'd been thinking along the same path. "Even more important," he added, "I don't want him to think I'm taking you away from him."

Irene's mind flashed back to her and Jeremy's first en-counter with Murdock. Who would have thought that bear of a man would turn out to be such excellent father mate-rial, she mused.

"Then I'll be leaving in the morning," Sarah said, pull-ing Irene's attention back to the present and her aunt. "I need to return to California and check on my house there. After that, I'm going to visit Aunt Ruth and Uncle Orville in Wyoming."

Irene studied her aunt with interest. "Going to see if some of those bridges you thought you'd burned aren't as irrep-arable as you'd thought?" she asked.

"I'm not sure why I'm going back," Sarah confessed. "I just feel like I need to."

"Just remember that you're always welcome here," Murdock interjected.

Jeremy yawned widely and Murdock grinned down at him. "Looks like it's time for you to go to bed, son."

"Sure, Dad," Jeremy replied with a happy smile.

* * *

Irene lay snuggled in Murdock's arms. She'd been lying there watching him sleep for a long time. They'd only been married for one month yet she was as comfortable with him as if he'd been in her life forever. For the first time since Jack's death she felt totally complete once again. Well, almost totally, she conceded, smiling softly.

"Morning," Murdock said, opening his eyes and seeing her.

"Morning," she replied.

His gaze narrowed. "Why do I have the feeling you have something on your mind?"

She flushed slightly, amazed by how easily he seemed to read her moods. "I guess because I do," she admitted, kissing him lightly.

"Are you going to tell me? Or am I going to have to torture it out of you?" he threatened, tickling her playfully.

"Stop that," she ordered between giggles. "I'll tell. I'll tell."

His tickling stopped. "I know I promised to respect your need for independence, but if something is bothering you and I can help, I want to."

"Actually your help is absolutely necessary in this instance," she replied. A slight flush of self-consciousness tinted her cheeks. "Jeremy's been hinting about wanting a little brother or sister. I don't want you to feel rushed. We don't have to do anything immediately." The love she felt for him, showed openly in her eyes. "But you are such a good father and I would like to have another child."

Murdock laughed a low, throaty, happy laugh. "Jeremy's been hinting about a sibling to me, too."

"And?" Irene coaxed, guessing from the grin on Murdock's face what his response had been but wanting to hear him tell her.

"I told him that if it was all right with you, it was all right with me." The brown of his eyes darkened with tenderness. "It's very all right with me." He moved his eyebrows up and down producing an exaggerated lecherous effect. "And I'm definitely going to enjoy doing my part."

Irene laughed. "I hoped you'd feel that way."

His hand moved along the curves of her body. "Now seems like as good a time as any to begin working on this project," he said, a husky quality entering his voice.

"Now feels like the perfect time," she agreed as his touch sparked desire.

*   *   *   *   *

Coming in February from

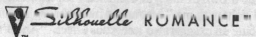

Silhouette ROMANCE™

Sister Switch

by
Carolyn Zane

When twin sisters switch identities, mischief, mayhem—and romance—are sure to follow!

UNWILLING WIFE
(FEB. '95 #1063)

Erica Brant agreed to take her sister's place as nanny for two rambunctious children. But she never considered that their handsome single father would want to make *her* his new bride!

WEEKEND WIFE
(MAY '95 #1082)

When a sexy stranger begged Emily Brant to pose as his wife for the weekend, it was an offer she couldn't resist. But what happens when she discovers he wants more than just a pretend marriage?

Don't miss the fun as the Brant sisters discover that trading places can lead to more than they'd ever imagined. SISTER SWITCH—only from Silhouette Romance!

Take 4 bestselling love stories FREE

Plus get a FREE surprise gift!

Get Ready to be Swept Away by
Silhouette's Spring Collection

Abduction & Seduction

These passion-filled stories explore both the dangerous
desires of men and the seductive powers of women.
Written by three of our most celebrated authors, they are
sure to capture your hearts.

Diana Palmer
Brings us a spin-off of her Long, Tall Texans series

Joan Johnston
Crafts a beguiling Western romance

Rebecca Brandewyne
New York Times bestselling author
makes a smashing contemporary debut

Available in March at your favorite retail outlet.

THIS SIDE OF HEAVEN

The miracle of love is waiting to be discovered
in Duncan, Oklahoma! Arlene James takes you there
in her miniseries, THIS SIDE OF HEAVEN.
Look for book four in February:

THE ROGUE WHO CAME TO STAY

Rodeo champ Griff Shaw had come home to Duncan to heal when he
found pretty single mom Joan Burton and her adorable daughter
living in his house! Griff wasn't about to turn Joan and her little girl
out, but did Joan dare share a roof with this rugged rogue?

Available in February, from

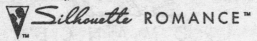

Silhouette ROMANCE™

SOH

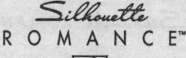

Those Harris boys are back in book three of...

WEDDING WAGER

by Sandra Steffen

Three sexy, single brothers bet they'll never say "I do." But the Harris boys are about to discover their vows of bachelor-hood don't stand a chance against the forces of love!

You met Mitch in BACHELOR DADDY #1028 (8/94) and Kyle in BACHELOR AT THE WEDDING #1045 (11/94). Now it's time for brother Taylor to take the marriage plunge in—

EXPECTANT BACHELOR #1056 (1/95): When Gina Jenson sets out to seduce the handsome Taylor, he's in for the surprise of his life. Because Gina wants him to father her child!

If you are looking for more titles by

ELIZABETH AUGUST

Don't miss this chance to order additional stories by one of Silhouette's great authors:

Silhouette Romance™

#08809	A SMALL FAVOR	$2.50	☐
#08833	THE COWBOY AND THE CHAUFFEUR	$2.59	☐
#08857	LIKE FATHER, LIKE SON	$2.69	☐
#08881	THE WIFE HE WANTED	$2.69	☐
	The following titles are part of the Smytheshire, Massachusetts miniseries		
#08921	THE VIRGIN WIFE	$2.69	☐
#08945	LUCKY PENNY	$2.75	☐
#08953	A WEDDING FOR EMILY	$2.75	☐
	(limited quantities available on certain titles)		

TOTAL AMOUNT	$
POSTAGE & HANDLING	$
($1.00 for one book, 50¢ for each additional)	
APPLICABLE TAXES*	$_____
<u>**TOTAL PAYABLE**</u>	$_____
(check or money order—please do not send cash)	

To order, complete this form and send it, along with a check or money order for the total above, payable to Silhouette Books, to: *In the U.S.*: 3010 Walden Avenue, P.O. Box 9077, Buffalo, NY 14269-9077; *In Canada*: P.O. Box 636, Fort Erie, Ontario, L2A 5X3.

Name: _____

Address: _____ City: _____

State/Prov.: _____ Zip/Postal Code: _____

*New York residents remit applicable sales taxes.
 Canadian residents remit applicable GST and provincial taxes.　　SEABACK3